ONE AND ONLY LOVE

STELLA MACLEAN

Cataloguing and Publication information is available from The Canadian ISBN Service System, Library and Archives Canada.

Title: One and Only Love/Stella MacLean

Identifiers:

ISBN: Print: 978-1-7381405-9-6

E-book: 978-1-7381405-8-9

Formatting Services: Sweet' N Spicy Designs

Cover Design: Sweet' N Spicy Designs

PROLOGUE

I t's wonderful to be back with you again. If you've read all my other stories, you know quite a bit about me. If this is your first one, I'm Helen Mason, a retired school teacher who lives in Spencer Island. These stories are about students I've taught over the years, people who went on to live good lives. There is something so special about being part of a young person's life as each of them learn and grow up to become really great people. I feel blessed.

This story is about Carolyn and Lucas Turner. They fell in love in high school, and graduated top of their class. Lucas was a computer genius who went away to take a degree in engineering, while Carolyn did an administration course at the local community college. They planned to marry and so they did, to the delight of their family and friends.

Carolyn is what I call an old-fashioned girl: love, marriage, followed by a house filled with children. As for Lucas, he wanted whatever Carolyn wanted. The perfect recipe for happiness it would seem…

But you'll see, life has a way of changing our plans, challenging how we think about life and changing our lives sometimes for better, sometimes for worse. They wanted to share their lives with children, to have a family and grow old together. In other words, they wanted it all.

But Carolyn and Lucas's road to happiness has not been as easy as it might have looked in the beginning, and their faith in each other would be tested, almost to the breaking point...

CHAPTER ONE

Sitting in his home office Lucas stared at the lawyer's letter, his thoughts racing. The private adoption they'd worked months on arranging wasn't going to happen. Lucas could hardly believe the words on the stark white paper. The mother had changed her mind.

He was disappointed, but his big worry was his wife Carolyn. How could he tell her their hope of a baby of their own wasn't going to be happen? How would he say the words that would break her heart? Could he delay telling her, at least for a while?

Yet, he knew that he could never keep a secret like this one. He couldn't face her knowing what he knew without sharing it with her.

He folded the letter and put it back in the envelope, his heart aching at what lay ahead for both of them. They could try again, maybe, but that could mean more disappointment. His heart ached for his wife as he thought about how to tell her. Yet, there was no good time to do this, he thought as he got up and went out to the kitchen where she was preparing lunch.

He'd known ever since he'd met her that Carolyn wanted a house filled with children. After they married, they tried to get pregnant until it was proven futile. The decision to adopt had not been easy, but they'd both agreed that it was the only option left to them.

He rested his elbow on the desk as he thought about his wife. She was everything he'd ever wanted: Bright, beautiful and caring. She'd been so brave through every step of the long process of trying to have a baby, while he'd become impatient and at times fed up with the whole thing. And at times his business had suffered due to the constant effort to get pregnant.

And with this letter, their hopes were once more dashed. He had to find the words to tell her, but not here in this house, a house with a baby's room all decorated and ready.

The only thing he could think of to do was to get her away from here, maybe convince her to come to Boston with him, to enjoy just a few hours of being together, happy and in love, before he broke the news.

He took a deep breath, put a smile on his face as he entered the kitchen. The sight of his wife, an apron tied around her waist, strands of hair trailing along her cheeks as she took the seafood chowder out of the oven, made him glad to be married to her. So glad. "Darling, I've got a proposition I know you won't be able to resist," he said.

"What's that? A trip to the UK? Venice at dusk?" she asked, as she pulled off her oven mitts, her smile lifting his spirits.

"You know I have to be in Boston tomorrow." He placed his arms around her. "You and I haven't had a trip away for so long. Why don't you come with me? We could stay overnight. Once I'm finished with business, we could have lunch, take a carriage ride around historic Boston, buy something for your garden at one of the stalls at the market. We've often talked about going into the city and spending time wandering the shops. Even better, why don't we do it today?" he asked, his eyes searching her face.

"Oh, Lucas, I want that, too. But I promised Celia that we'd meet for lunch. Her decorating firm wants to showcase our nursery in one of her magazine ads. They did all the colors and helped me choose all the extras for the baby's room."

Carolyn snuggled closer to him. He soaked in her smile, felt the old pull of attraction that had been there between them since the day they'd met in high school.

He didn't want to tell her about the letter, here in the house where they'd expected to be bringing home a new baby. There had to be some way to convince her to come to Boston with him. "Why don't I book a suite at the Parker House Inn? We could go out to dinner, or order room service, a bottle of wine, just the two of us. We haven't stayed downtown in Boston in years. Would that convince you to come with me?"

"A night in Boston?" she asked.

"Or two nights, if you'd like. Beautiful surroundings, all the amenities. Think fluffy robes, nothing on under them. Pure luxury in a suite all to ourselves. Me reaching for you," he whispered in her ear, hearing her breath quicken as his body hardened.

He kissed her lips, felt her body curve into his. His blood hot, his body arching toward hers, he felt her move against him. "What do you say?"

"I would do anything for you, Lucas Caldwell Turner," she said, her lips on his throat, her breath searing his skin.

"And me for you," he whispered, pulling her toward the stairs and their bedroom.

Her quick intake of breath was all he needed. He continued to kiss her as they moved up the stairs. "If you come with me to Boston, I promise you the best time you've ever had, Mrs. Turner."

He followed her into the bedroom.

They lay down together. He eased his hands over her tummy, down along her hips, hugging her body against his. "What do you say?"

She looked deep into his eyes, her lips parted, her hair fanned out across the pillow. "You never cease to amaze me," she whispered, her fingers continuing their course over his cheek, down his neck.

"How so?" he asked, loving this game, this moment when she would succumb to him. It had always been that way.

"I agree we need to get away, time to ourselves. It would be really nice to spend a couple days in Boston. You win, my love. I'll cancel my lunch date."

He knew they'd have to find time to talk about the letter, but first they needed a few moments of happiness untouched by all the things going on around getting pregnant. He wanted just a few more hours of not thinking about anything but each other.

He kissed her, cradling her head in his hands. "Thank you. You won't regret going with me. Besides, how can you resist the chance to have me all to yourself?" he teased, aware of the times he'd wanted her to go away with him when he'd be gone for days without her, and she'd remained at home, either for a doctor's appointment, or all the planning around decorating the baby's room.

"Lucas, I love you," she whispered as her body writhed under his caress, a groan of pleasure escaping her lips.

"And I love you," he murmured against her skin as he held her. "Why don't we leave now?" he asked, suddenly wanting to be away from the house and the pain the letter would cause his wife. "Let's just escape to a lovely hotel and forget all our responsibilities."

She glanced up at him. "Why not?"

Two hours later, he and Carolyn arrived in Boston. "Why don't I drop you somewhere along King Street, give you a little time to shop? And before you say anything about the cost, I want you to buy whatever you want. Promise me you'll do that," he said.

She was confident that this trip was meant to be. The next couple of days together would work its magic on them. She'd never stayed at the Parker House Inn, but she'd looked on the Internet and was blown away by the gorgeous rooms. "I promise to buy whatever I see that I like," she offered, stroking his arm.

"Perfect. I'll call you the second I'm out of my meeting and we'll go for a late lunch," he said, navigating the tight lanes of traffic leading toward Washington Street, the hallmark of Boston civility.

"I wish we'd planned to do this with Brad and Maria. She's such a great shopper, and we always have a good time together. I was never so happy as when he arrived back from a business trip to Concord to tell me he'd met the woman of his dreams. Do you think they'll get married? I mean, Brad talks about her all the time, and I want my brother to be as happy as we are."

"Brad and Maria are not on my mind at all. They have their life and we have ours," he said, his gaze direct, a small furrow forming between his eyes as he turned to her. "All I want is to let the world go away and you and I to focus on us," he said as he maneuvered the large SUV into a narrow parking spot.

"Okay. No more talk about anyone or anything but us," she said. She didn't want anything to ruin their mini vacation. Reaching across the wide console, she squeezed his hand where it rested on the steering wheel. "I can't wait for you to be finished. You're right. We need to get away. Starting today, we'll plan to do something like this once a month. We deserve time alone together, don't we?"

"Exactly. Why can't we just take off, act like a pair of teenagers in love? The way we used to do," he said, his smile intimate, wrapping around her, signaling that whatever was bothering him had gone. She knew him so well. She'd seen the tight lines around his mouth, the look of anxiety in his eyes.

Kissing him quickly, she said, "After I'm done shopping, I'll call a cab and go to the inn. I'll check in and be waiting for you. I'm going to buy something really sexy to wear tonight." She kissed him again before she reached for the door handle. "You'd better be ready," she teased, seeing the love in his eyes, her body tingled. "I'll order a bottle of champagne to the room."

He pulled her to him and kissed her, his mouth moving over hers in a way that made her weak with desire. "I can't wait, woman." His smile radiated happiness as his lips claimed hers. "I'll see you later. We'll order room service and you can model your latest purchase...before I remove it."

Five hours later, Lucas lay sprawled on the bed, Carolyn in his arms, the sheets crumpled around them, his need for her completely sated.

"You are the most beautiful woman in the world," he said, his throat filled with emotion as unexpected tears tingled behind his lids. He hadn't felt this way for a very long time. He'd come to the inn and been met at the door of their suite by his wife dressed in a skimpy lace item that covered just enough and hinted at a lot more. He'd fallen into bed with her, and they'd had the best afternoon of lovemaking he could remember.

Slowly he kissed her lips, his fingers caressing her cheek. "I've never loved anyone the way I love you."

She returned his kiss. "I love you, too, so much," she whispered, her gaze on him and only him.

"I've missed this," he said, his heart filled to overflowing.

"What do you mean?" She toyed with the hair on his chest.

"The way we made love, the closeness, the sheer excitement of simply enjoying each other."

She pulled back a little. "But we've always been like this with each other."

He placed his fingers gently over her lips to silence her. "Not like this. Not with this intensity and simply for the sheer pleasure of being with each other."

Her gaze never left his face, and he saw the shimmer of unshed tears in her eyes.

"I don't mean to say we haven't made love to each other these past years, but there was always the other...."

Lucas wished he'd said nothing. "I'm sorry. I shouldn't have said anything. It's just that I feel like I have you back. The Carolyn I married and have loved for so long. That's all I meant."

"I understand," she said, her voice wistful.

"Then let's not think about anything other than ourselves for the next two days. If I have my way, we won't leave this room. We won't need to." He leaned up on one elbow and smiled at her. "I don't ever want to leave this bed, but I am a little hungry. Why don' I order room service? Another bottle of champagne, even?" He winked at her.

Carolyn chuckled. "You think you'll get me a little tipsy and have your way with me again?"

"You're tempting me, again," he said, kissing her, feeling the heat rise, the tremble of her lips against his.

"I hope so," she whispered, her hands moving over his chest, feeding his desire.

He held her close, his mouth claiming hers, his hands spreading across her back, moving down her body, her answering intake of breath music to his ears. "Yes," he whispered against her lips. "We will put food on hold for a while longer."

The evening was perfect. They ordered room service, a spectacular meal with a bottle of champagne. They spent the rest of the evening making love. After Carolyn fell asleep in his arms he fought with himself as to when best to tell her about the letter. He wanted to forget about the letter and just spend time with his wife, but he knew he had to tell her.

CHAPTER TWO

The next day dawned bright and sunny. They took a carriage ride around historic Boston, ate crab cakes with sparkling wine at a tiny bistro overlooking the market. They talk about so many things; about his work, about the hours she's spent working on the nursery, her love of gardening. She brought up the planned adoption, forcing him to look away so that he wouldn't see what was in his eyes. A stark reminder that he had to tell her about the letter.

When the returned to the suite, they made love again. He hadn't been this happy in he didn't know how long. Between his work and the need to get pregnant, it hadn't been an easy time. And even now, as happy as he was, he had to talk to her about the letter...and break her heart.

He didn't want to tell her. He didn't want to hurt her. But she had to know.

The sooner, the better.

He eased from the bed, and went to get the letter out of his jacket pocket. He felt her eyes on him, and he'd never felt more anxious in his life. "I got this letter in the mail," he said, bringing it over to her.

"What is it?" she asked, smiling as she looked up at him. "A letter?"

She jumped up. "The adoption! We're getting a baby!" she cried, pulling the letter from his hand and tearing the envelope, gripping the letter in her hands, her face radiant.

He watched as she read, her expression going from elation to shock. "Oh, Lucas, this can't be true. It can't be," she said, looking up at him, the color drained from her cheeks. "This cannot be true."

"I'm afraid it is, my love," he said, pulling her into his arms, and cradling her head against his chest. Gently he took the letter from her hands, and eased her back on the bed. He covered them both with the sheet, as he listened to his wife's quiet sobs, his heart a hard lump in his chest. How would Carolyn ever get over this? She'd been counting on this child the lawyer had found for them. She'd talked of nothing else for months.

Carolyn couldn't believe this was happening. They'd tried so hard to have a baby, done all the testing, finally succumbed to the idea they wouldn't have a baby of their own and had arranged to adopt. She'd been so sure the adoption would go through. Everyone told them they were the perfect couple to adopt. She clung to Lucas, her body trembling, her heart thudding in her chest.

"Lucas, how could this happen? Why did the woman change her mind?"

"We knew there was always that possibility," he said, stroking her hair, holding her close in his arms.

"How long have you known?" she asked.

"The letter came yesterday. I couldn't keep it from you, but I wanted us to have a few happy moments before I told you. I'm so sorry. I don't know what we can do about it. Maybe try again."

"Oh, Lucas, I love you for not telling me. For letting me have a wonderful time here," she said, wrapping her arm across his chest, feeling the warmth of his skin, a safe haven. "But we need to figure out if there's anything we can do. Can we make an appointment with the lawyer, see what he says?"

"We will when we get back home." He hugged her close.

The chime of his cell phone startled him. "What?"

"I thought you turned your phone off," she said, stirring gently against him.

"I did, too," he said clicking it off.

A few moments later the room phone rang.

Carolyn sighed. "What now?"

"It must be important, or maybe it's the inn wondering if we need anything. Either way," he said, reaching for the sleek black phone on the bedside table, "I'll take care of it." He picked up the phone.

"Lucas, it's Nancy. Sorry to interrupt, but I've had an urgent call from a lawyer in Concord. He insists on talking to you now. He's on the other line."

Lucas looked over at Carolyn. "Brad looks after our clients in Concord. Did he say what he wanted?"

"No. Just that he needed to talk to you in person as soon as possible. There seems to be some sort of emergency."

"Work," he whispered, placing his fingers on her lips. "Tell whoever it is to call Brad."

"I did, but he said it's a personal matter, that he needs to speak to you directly."

"Okay, put him on," Lucas said with a sigh, pulling Carolyn closer as he settled in to hear what the man had to say.

"Hello, is this Lucas Turner?" a deep, gruff voice inquired.

"It is. What is so urgent that you need to speak to me

today? I'll be back in the office on Monday and we can talk then."

"I'm afraid that won't work. I have to ask you a few questions," the man said.

"Who is this?" Lucas said, annoyed at the man's presumption that he could dictate to him.

The phone was silent for a few moments. "It's Larry Knowles. I'm the attorney for Deidre MacPherson."

Deidre MacPherson? "I'm sorry," Lucas said, his mind scrambling over the possibilities. Deidre had never attempted to contact him after their long-ago weekend together. "Why are you calling me? I have no connection to that person."

"Ms. MacPherson was killed in an automobile accident on Thursday. According to her will, you are sole beneficiary of her estate with the proviso that you become the legal guardian of her daughter, Summer."

Lucas swung his legs over the side of the bed and sat up. "You've got the wrong person. This is a mistake."

"Not according to what I'm reading here." He could hear the rustle of pages and a short pause. "She states that you are Summer's father. She wants you to be her daughter's guardian and to adopt her as soon as possible. When you do, you will receive the total of her estate worth over five million dollars. Her will is very clear on this point. Did you have no idea that she'd done this?"

It wasn't possible. He couldn't be the father of Deidre's child. They'd spent a weekend together. Nothing more. He'd tried unsuccessfully for years to get his wife pregnant. What was the likelihood that he'd fathered a child with another woman?

The story had to be a lie. Obviously, Deidre had decided to make him responsible for a child he'd never met and couldn't possibly have fathered. He took a deep breath. "I have no idea what you're talking about. I think this conversation has gone far enough," he said forcefully, his eyes meeting Carolyn's anxious expression as she snuggled against him, the gentle touch of her hand offering him support.

"I have here a document, a DNA test that Ms. MacPherson had done on her child and you. You are the father of Summer Leigh MacPherson. We need to talk. When can you be in Concord, Mr. Turner?"

"There has to be a mistake. I don't know what you're talking about," Lucas said, his heart shrinking in his chest. What the lawyer said simply wasn't true. It had been years ago, another lifetime, and none of it had meant anything to him. Carolyn knew nothing about that weekend, had never questioned any of his business trips.

His wife was a Christian who believed that the truth was a guiding principle in life. He believed it, too. He hadn't wanted to lie to her about that weekend, and so had pleaded a heavy workload in Concord.

He didn't want to lie to her now, but he had no choice. If she found out that he'd fathered a child while they were trying to get pregnant, she would be devastated. He had no doubt that she would leave him. He couldn't let that happen. Not over a mistake he had always regretted.

It had nothing to do with their life now. Carolyn's happiness meant everything to him. He glanced furtively at his wife, seeing a look of confusion on her face, wishing he could end the call and it would all simply go away.

"What's going on?" she asked, sitting up straighter, slipping away from his side.

He had to do something to save the situation before he was forced to use words that would cause Carolyn to be suspicious. "Look, Mr. Knowles. We can discuss this on Monday. I'm sure there is some misunderstanding. We'll clear it up then."

"That won't work. This child, your daughter, is living with her nanny, but arrangements need to be made for her. There is no immediate family, and if you don't take the little girl, other arrangements will have to be made. I need to see you tomorrow. I'll be in my office. What time can you be here?"

"I can't drop everything just because you want to meet," Lucas said, trying to make sense of this, but even more, trying to absorb that he was supposedly the father of a child he'd never known existed.

He scrubbed his face in disbelief.

CHAPTER THREE

At the sudden change in Lucas's voice, a chill ran through Carolyn. Something was horribly, terribly wrong. She'd never seen Lucas look so awful, so confused and uncertain in all the years she'd known him. "Honey, what is it?"

Carolyn watched his anxious expression as fear wrapped around her heart, blocking the air from her lungs. Had someone been hurt? Was it a friend? Someone at work? Brad? It couldn't be her brother, could it? The way Lucas's gaze moved around the room, never connecting with hers, was terrifying. Unable to help herself, she reached up to put her arms around his shoulders, needing to learn more with each passing minute. "What is going on, Lucas? What is it?"

Clutching the phone tighter to his ear, he turned away from her. "If you insist, I will be there tomorrow afternoon. Not a minute before. Whatever's going on here, I'm as anxious as you to get to the bottom of it."

Relief whistled through her at his words, the strict business tone he used. From what he said, it was clear that no one was hurt or in trouble, at least, no one she knew. Yet the soft light from the window exposed the pallor of Lucas's skin. "What's wrong, honey?" she whispered urgently.

"It's nothing, a misunderstanding that needs to be cleared up, that's all," he said, hanging up.

"What sort of misunderstanding?" she asked.

"Someone died and I'm needed in Concord tomorrow."

His tone was matter-of-fact, his expression grim, making her even more curious. She'd never known Lucas to respond to someone's death with such consternation. It was as if he didn't believe what he'd been told. "That's awful. I'm sorry. But why did they call you? If it's about business, why didn't they call Brad?"

He shook his head, still holding the phone as he rose from the bed and went to the window.

She followed him, taking his hand, she said, "Whatever's going on, I want to be there with you. Tell me who died."

"It's someone...I knew... A client."

"Someone you knew? In Concord?"

Lucas turned away, moving closer to the heavily draped window, his shoulders slumped.

She waited. He didn't turn back to her, seek her out the way he did when something was bothering him. He'd been like that since the day they'd met. She could always rely on him to share his thoughts, whatever they were, good or bad.

"That was a call informing me about the death of Deidre MacPherson, the CEO of one of our major clients in Concord. It seems I'm needed there urgently. Tomorrow at the latest." He scrubbed his face with his hands.

The set of his shoulders, the way he didn't seem to see her or even be aware of her, made Carolyn realize that, for the first time in their marriage, he was keeping something from her. He'd hidden things from her before, like a surprise birthday party or when he gave her diamond earrings on their seventh anniversary. But they were surprises, not lies.

18

And this was a lie. She didn't understand how she knew that. She'd never been suspicious of Lucas, had always trusted him completely. But now it was clear that there was something he was concealing, something so important to him that he was willing to lie to her about it. Her stomach lurched. "Lucas, what is going on? I'm your wife. You owe me an explanation."

"That was her lawyer. He needs to talk to me." Lucas glanced around, spotted his underwear and awkwardly pulled them on, all the while never once glancing in her direction.

"About what? And why you?" she insisted, though her heart pounded so hard in her ears she could barely hear.

"That woman, the one who died..." He searched the room for his shirt and pants. "She left her entire estate to me."

"Why would a woman leave you money?"

"Because." Lucas grabbed his clothes and got dressed hurriedly. His look when he met her eyes was one of agony and despair. "Because she's crazy. She claims that she had a child. That the child is mine. I haven't seen her in five years. I have no idea why she thinks her child is mine."

Carolyn couldn't breathe. She reached out to the drapes to support her as her knees began to buckle. His words cascaded over her, blocking her thoughts, filling her with disbelief and panic. "What are you talking about?" There had to be a mistake. Lucas and she couldn't have children. All the testing proved that. She searched his face, seeking some sort of denial from him. "Tell me this isn't true. This can't be true. You can't have a baby."

"Carolyn, you need to sit down," he said as he came to her, pulled her into his arms and led her to the sofa near the fire-place. "Let me try to explain what I believe is going on."

"Did you have an affair with her?" she asked, her body shaking at the enormity of it all. Lucas in another woman's bed. Lucas making love to another woman, his hands, his body on hers. The intimacy of the act, the love he was capable of making to Carolyn offered to another woman. "Tell me the truth!" she demanded, feeling sick to her stomach.

"Carolyn! I'm sorry. Really sorry." He went down on one knee in front of her, his eyes pleading, his voice filled with remorse.

"Five years ago?" She heard a scream and realized it was hers. "You had an affair five years ago when we were trying to have a baby?"

"Not an affair. Never." He covered his face with his hands. "You and I were going through a rough time. I was alone, working hard, worried about you, about us."

Her mind fumbled over his words. Her husband, the man she loved, had had an affair with another woman. He'd broken a solemn vow to her, one he'd taken before God. This couldn't be true. But hadn't he just admitted to it? "When? When did you do this?"

"Back when I managed our clients in Concord. Before Brad took over."

"Is that why Brad started going there? Does he know about this?"

"No one knows. It was just one weekend, and I've regretted it ever since." He stared at the ceiling, then back at her. "I've never regretted anything more in my whole life."

There were tears in his eyes, but it didn't matter. Tears could not change what he'd just admitted to. "Regretted it," she echoed. "You had sex with her and you regretted it." She struggled to sort out her thoughts.

"I swear I did not know she had a child. And I *know* it isn't mine. I wouldn't...couldn't."

"Stop! You just admitted to having sex with a woman who had a child. Your child.

"No! Not my child!"

He scrubbed his face. "Carolyn, please don't do this. It can't be my child." He touched her bare leg. "You saw the test results."

"But why would she lie? Why would she leave her entire estate to you if you weren't the father of her child?"

"I have no idea...but maybe she decided that I'd make the best father." He clutched at the idea. "Maybe the real father wasn't parent material. Everyone in the Concord office knew we were trying to get pregnant. I had to give some explanation when I'd have to rush back here. Maybe she figured I'd jump at the chance to be the father of her child."

She got up and walked around, letting his words sink in. "No woman would do that, would she?"

"If she wanted to provide for her daughter in the event of something happening to her, what better father than a man wanting to have a family?"

Lucas watched her as she paced. "I don't know anything, only that I love you and this is...is not possible."

For a fraction of a second, she almost went to him, to console him the way she always had. But she couldn't. He'd hurt her so badly. But despite the horror of another woman, he had been tested and he couldn't have a child. "If this is not your child, a DNA test will prove you're not the father, won't it?"

"Yes. It will. It certainly will."

"This man. This Mr. Knowles said he has DNA proof. But I don't believe it. We, you and I, can't have children, and so this has to be some sort of awful mistake."

She gathered her clothes, and got dressed, her hands shaking so bad, she dropped her earrings on the floor. Lucas grabbed them from where they landed on the plush cream carpet. "I gave these to you. They're your favorites."

"I don't want jewelry bought out of guilt," she said,

striding into the bathroom. She combed her fingers through her hair, applied a little blush and gathered her cosmetics bag. She may just have been totally humiliated by her husband, but she would not leave the suite without looking in control and in charge.

In the bedroom, she shoved the remainder of her things into her suitcase. So many thoughts were crashing around her mind, each delivering yet another blow to her self-esteem. "If this is true, it means that I'm the one who can't have children, doesn't it?"

"Carolyn, please don't do this."

"I have no choice. I've waited our entire marriage for a baby, and now someone is claiming you're the father of her child."

"Carolyn, honey, I recognize this is hard for you. I wish I didn't have to bring it up," he said, his head lowered, his expression downcast.

"But you did and now I have to deal with it. How could you do this? To cheat on me, on us, is unbearable."

"Carolyn, we love each other. I've hurt you and I will make it up to you somehow. I should have told you about the weekend with Deidre, but I didn't want to hurt you over nothing. And it was nothing. Just a mindless fling because I was feeling so isolated and alone in our marriage. But that's no excuse. I broke the promise I made to you. Please understand I never meant to hurt you. You, of all people. I love you, Carolyn." His face was ashen, his eyes pleading.

"Is it a girl or a boy?" she asked, feeling nothing, as if her body were floating off somewhere, that none of this was real.

"It's a girl," he said, his voice flat, as if the realization hadn't yet dawned on him that he was a father.

"How old is she?" Carolyn demanded.

Lucas glanced around the room his hands shoved deep into his pockets. "I guess she'd be four or so."

"If it's true, what do you intend to do about her?" Carolyn asked.

Lucas gave a long sigh. "You and I both know I'm not the father. I made a mistake, but the child can't be mine."

"If you're so sure the child is not yours, maybe you should take our lawyer with you," Carolyn said, trying to sound reasonable and in control even as her heart crumpled in her chest.

"Maybe I should take our lawyer, but first I'd like to see for myself what's going on." He rubbed his palms together. "I know it's asking a lot, but would you go with me to Concord?"

She was halfway to the door when he said the words. She stopped and turned around so quickly her overnight bag banged into the back of her leg, delivering a stinging blow.

"Me? You're asking me to go with you? You want me to help you solve a problem all of your making."

Instantly, he was at her side. "It was a stupid mistake. I take full responsibility for it."

She stepped away, her back straight, her eyes boring into him. "Then you can go to Concord and sort this mess out."

"Carolyn, what I did has hurt you. I want to make it up to you, but first we have to find out what is going on, what this lawyer wants. As for Deidre, I was in Concord working with a client, working hard and wishing I could be home with you, instead."

"A client? You mean this Deidre MacPherson person?" Carolyn asked, trying to decide how much longer she could stand to be near him, knowing what he'd done to her.

Lucas held her shoulders, his touch gentle and kind, the way he always behaved when he wanted her to understand something going on with his work Without warning, the time he'd come to her, telling her they'd have to mortgage their home in order to meet a loan payment flashed in front of her. The threat that they might lose their home had been one of the worst moments of her life. To lose her home meant she would lose the place she dreamed of raising their children.

"Yes, it was Deidre MacPherson's business. She had just landed a major contract and we were providing technical support. I had to stay over the weekend with my technicians to get the system up and running. We went out to celebrate and something happened. I never saw her again or had any form of contact. I swear."

"I don't want to hear it!" She glared at him, gritting her teeth.

He stepped back. "I didn't mean to remind you... All I want you to know is that I have nothing to hide where she is concerned."

The warmth of Lucas's body mingled with his cologne, filling her nostrils, and for a few pain-filled moments she wished they could simply forget everything that had happened and go back to bed. Feeling deflated and faced with the anguish in his eyes, she relented a little. "I thought our marriage was sound. That we were good. I don't know you anymore."

"Please don't say that. I've gotten us into a terrible mess. And I will find a way out of it, if only you'll give me a little time to make things right," he said, his voice shaking.

Lucas looked into her eyes, into the depths of her, her heart and her soul. They had always had this connection, this one-to-one sensation whenever they spoke about those things close to their hearts. She wanted to reach out to him, to soothe him, but the agony of what he'd done left her feeling so betrayed she want to run away. She couldn't touch him knowing that another woman had touched him, probably in much the same way. "I don't want to deal with this, any of this."

"Neither do I, but this man won't stop trying. And it might be better if we faced this head-on, like we would with any crisis in our lives. What do you think?" He held his breath. His gaze searched her face.

"What if we go and he has irrefutable proof that it's your child?"

Once again, his hands reached for hers. She hugged herself, not letting him touch her.

"Carolyn, think about it. If I was the father of her child, why didn't she tell me? I can't help but believe that she would have wanted me to know, to share the responsibility for the baby, the cost of her education, all the things that are needed to care for a child. I can't imagine that she wouldn't have insisted that I help out. What woman wouldn't?"

"What will we do if it is your child?" Carolyn asked, as she kept waiting to wake up from a bad dream, cry out and be cuddled by her husband, the way it had happened after other nightmares.

Lucas stood perfectly still. "It isn't my child."

If she was to keep her marriage as God intended, and rebuild the trust they'd always shared, she had to work her way through this horrible mess. "There is only one way I will consider being involved with you in this, and that is if you tell me everything. If 1 find out you've been lying to me about this woman, about your time with her, our marriage is over."

"I have told you the truth. Someone made a mistake in the testing."

She stood with her hand on the door, her head pounding, and watched her husband's face. A face she loved, had loved most of her life. And now, because of one phone call, it might all be over.

"Carolyn, I'm begging you to go with me. You can't imagine how terrible I feel for the pain I've caused you. I want to make it up to you by being totally honest about all this. From now on, wherever this takes us, I want you with me."

She heard the sincerity in his voice, saw the expression of remorse on his face, and her determination to walk out slipped from her. Whatever he'd done, however much he'd hurt her, she was still his wife and she had to allow him to make this right. Maybe he couldn't, and she would have to live with that. But whatever came out of this, she didn't want to end up regretting what she'd done, how she'd behaved.

As she stared at him, memories of their life flashed before her eyes, all the good times they'd had together would end up being for nothing if she acted too rashly. Deep down inside she wanted to believe that, despite everything, they might still have a chance.

"I don't know if I can do this, any of it. You've hurt me in ways I could never have imagined. Right now, I hate you, and I can't imagine ever getting over what I'm feeling."

"Carolyn, I'm so afraid," he said, his hands working at his sides.

"Would you be willing to go for marriage counseling?" she asked.

"Of course. All I want is you, Carolyn. I want us to find each other again, to feel what we've felt all these years."

She looked at the man she'd married over ten years ago, at the light dusting of freckles on his cheeks, the way his eyes seemed to see straight through her. Was it possible that somehow their marriage would survive this? Love didn't die easily. She'd seen her parents' marriage and the trouble they'd gone through, the loss of faith when her dad's gambling problem had nearly bankrupted the family. She had to believe that her marriage would survive this, that marriage counseling might help them regain the trust they'd lost.

But she had no idea how. And if it turned out that Lucas

had been more involved with this woman than he said, it could be the final blow to their marriage, something that Carolyn would never get over. Part of her found it simply unbelievable that her husband could have fathered a child when they'd done everything to have one of their own.

Carolyn took a deep breath to ease the headache building. "Okay. I will go with you."

He eased her gently into his arms. "I love you, Carolyn. So much," he said, tears streaming down his cheeks, his shoulders shaking.

"We'll get through this," he whispered close to her ear. "There is nothing we can't do if we put our minds to it. I made a mistake, but I'm willing to make it up to you. As for the child, there is no way that little girl is mine. And I'll prove it by having the DNA testing redone in a reputable lab."

"I agree," she said, her voice low as she looked into his eyes.

"This is one giant mistake on someone's part, and I'll prove it." He put his arm around her shoulders and led her to the sofa. "I should never have told you about Deidre the way I did. It was thoughtless and hurtful. There's nothing I can do to fix that, but if you'll go with me while we establish that I'm not the father, then we can work on us."

"I hope so," she whispered.

Lucas saw the misery in his wife's eyes and his heart contracted in his chest. How could he have done this to her? "Carolyn, I have been so damned stupid. You deserve better than what I've given you by way of explanation. I'm sorry about everything, but most of all I'm sorry for causing you such pain. "Thank you for agreeing to come with me. And I promise you that we will figure this out."

. . .

The next day they drove to Concord. It would have been so pleasant if not for the impending meeting. Lucas had lain awake for hours wondering how the DNA test showed him to be the father. And if he was the father, why hadn't Deidre told him? No woman would want to go through a birth and the raising of a child without some sort of family support.

And why had she done the test if she didn't plan to tell him? Had she had a relationship with another man and wanted to be certain that he couldn't claim the child? She was obviously a rich woman. Had a man she'd dated tried to say the child was his?

The lawyer hadn't said how old the little girl was. Maybe she was too young to be his daughter. He knew the exact weekend he'd spent with Deidre, so if the child had been born more than nine months after that, she couldn't be his. Had Deidre appointed him guardian because she thought he would do what he could for her daughter, regardless of whether or not he was the father?

As he mulled it all over, he could not understand her motivations. No matter how he looked at it, he couldn't figure out why she would keep the paternity of her daughter a secret, yet name him as the child's father in her will. It made zero sense. Even if Deidre was trying to prevent another man from gaining custody of the child, there were more effective and less destructive ways to do so.

For now, he would concentrate on the road ahead and trying to ease Carolyn's concerns about what they'd face at the lawyer's office. "I booked us into the nicest inn around the area. Might as well enjoy being comfortable while we get this over with."

He glanced at her, at the way her hair fell around her cheeks, at her beautiful lips and the set of her chin. All features he was intimately acquainted with and loved about her. He squeezed her hand. "We're going to be fine. This will be settled easily. I'll have our lawyer look after the details of a second DNA test and then we'll head back home. When we get home I'd like us to plan a trip to Europe. We've talked about it, but now I think we should do it. We've earned our time away to explore all those places we learned about in school. What do you say?"

"Lucas, I can't talk about a trip right now."

"But all this doesn't change the fact that we deserve a wonderful trip away from here, from my business and all that it entails. I'm also offering you the shopping trip of a lifetime anywhere in Europe you'd like to go. You'll have a chance to shop to your heart's content. Will you think about it?"

"Let's get this meeting over first," Carolyn said, her lips set in a firm line.

She didn't touch his arm as she often did when they were driving together. He missed her touch, the way it made him feel so loved.

They drove into downtown Concord to the address they had for the law office. It was an elegant older home just off the main street with a wide verandah and tall white columns flanking the entranceway. Upon entering the cool, open foyer, they were greeted by a woman wearing an impeccable navy suit. She smiled at them as she introduced herself and led them to a quiet, high-ceilinged room at the rear of the building. "Mr. Knowles will be with you momentarily. Is there anything I can get either of you? A coffee perhaps? Soft drink?"

"Nothing for me," Lucas said as Carolyn shook her head.

Lucas focused on the space to keep his mind from what was about to happen. The wood paneling and large window, with teal satin drapes that looked out into the back garden, dominated the room. There was no desk, only an antique table and chair placed along the wall near the window. The opposite wall contained a credenza that spanned its length. "This isn't your typical lawyer's office," Lucas said to overcome the hushed silence of the room.

"This must be one of those boutique law firms that specializes in estate work," Carolyn said, remaining where she'd stood since they walked into the room.

He came toward her, his arms aching to wrap her in his embrace. "You okay? You were pretty quiet in the car."

She shrugged.

The door opened and a man entered, his navy tailored suit and gold tie a perfect accent for the room, his dark hair and mustache impeccable. "I'm Larry Knowles. So glad you could make it today," he said without shaking hands. "Shall we get started?" he asked, pointing to the two chairs across from the table. He smoothed his tie as he sat. "Mr. Turner, as I explained on the phone, you have been named by Ms. MacPherson to be guardian of her only daughter. She has left very clear instructions as to how this will be worked out."

"Please stop right there. My wife and I, for personal reasons, do not believe that I am the biological parent of this child. We want the DNA test done by a reputable lab of our choosing before we go any further with this discussion."

Larry Knowles sat back in his chair, a surprised look on his face. "DNA is conclusive proof as far as I'm aware."

"That's assuming that the samples gathered were handled correctly, and that the lab followed strict procedures. I am not aware as to how or where my DNA was collected, and if it was collected in such a way to establish it was mine. It certainly was done without my permission. How have you determined that the DNA used to establish paternity was, in fact, mine?" he asked.

"It's true that I cannot personally vouch for the authenticity of the sample. Of course, I'm relying on Ms. MacPherson's information," the lawyer said, showing his first moment of uncertainty.

"Then it only seems right to me, given how much is at stake, that the testing be done again. I'm sure there is lots of Ms. MacPherson's DNA still present in her home, and I'm willing to provide a fresh sample for examination."

Larry Knowles looked straight at Lucas, started to say something, then stopped. He glanced quickly at Carolyn, then back to Lucas. "I have no reason whatsoever to doubt Deidre MacPherson. She was a friend as well as a client. But I do see your point. My only wish is that you do it as quickly as possible. Summer is living in her home with her nanny, and this needs to be resolved."

"What happens to Summer when it is proven that my husband isn't the father?" Carolyn asked.

"You have to understand that Deidre was absolutely positive that your husband was the father of her little girl. Having no close family she wanted to give her daughter to, she chose the biological father as guardian in the event Deidre didn't live to see her child grow to adulthood. If, for whatever reason, your husband doesn't take the child, she will be a ward of the state, which means that foster care will have to be arranged," the lawyer said.

"Are you certain there is no family for her?" Lucas asked. "None at all?"

"A cousin who is in her sixties." The lawyer glanced from one to the other. "Look, I know this is a shock for both of you. And I understand you feel there has been a serious mistake made. If you'll give me the name of the lab you want to deal with, I will make arrangements for Summer to be tested along with you. But in the meantime, Deidre had one more request."

"What is it?" Lucas asked, suddenly afraid that it might be some sort of burial request since she had no family. He didn't want to put Carolyn through anything more than was necessary.

"Deidre put together a video of Summer's life over the past four years. It's simply a visual portrait of a little girl who was the light of her mother's life. They were very close and Summer is a beautiful little girl. Deidre wasn't certain how you'd respond to her last wishes and so she requested that you watch the video before you left my office. It won't take long."

He opened a drawer and brought out a laptop, setting it on the desk in front of Lucas and Carolyn. A few clicks and the screen glowed blue before the picture of a newborn appeared. "I'll leave you to watch the video and be back in a few minutes."

Unable to stop himself, Lucas leaned toward the screen. Slowly photos emerged, showing an infant asleep in her car seat, followed by her first steps and her wide smile, dressed in a Halloween teddy bear costume. A woman's voice, carefully modulated, yet warm and upbeat, filled the room.

"Is that Deidre speaking?" Carolyn asked.

A chill ran along his shoulders. It felt as if Deidre were in the room. "Yes, I believe so... It's been a while." He would have recognized her voice anywhere. It was such a distinct mix of Southern drawl combined with a New England twang.

"The child is sweet." Carolyn sighed. "How lucky she was to have such a beautiful baby girl."

Slowly the images shifted to show the home she lived in, the front steps and the street in front of Deidre's house. There were closer shots showing Summer's rosy complexion and her glossy red curls. Lucas recognized the backgrounds in the photos all were places around Deidre's home and office.

Carolyn took his hand. "Have you seen any of these before?"

"No. Never," Lucas said as the video showed Summer in a pink party dress, her red curls framing her face. There was something so familiar about her, about the way she cocked her head and smiled at the camera. Deidre could be heard in the background wishing Summer a happy third birthday.

The camera panned close in. Summer's face filled the screen. Lucas stared for a minute, slowly becoming aware of something he couldn't mistake for anything other than what it was.

"Lucas. Look!" Carolyn cried. "She's got the same cleft in her chin as you have. And her smile. Oh, God. Lucas. Her smile is yours."

Lucas swallowed. She did have his chin... "Let's not jump to conclusions." He moved his chair closer to Carolyn's and pulled her hand into his lap. "This little girl is beautiful, but she could be anyone's little girl," he said, unable to grasp the truth of what he'd seen a few minutes ago.

The next photo was of Summer hugging a large teddy bear. Deidre's voice could be heard once again. "Lucas, if you're watching this, it means I am gone. I need you to care for our daughter. I had the DNA testing done just a few months after Summer was born. There is no doubt that you're the father. Summer has your smile, your curls and that cute little cleft in her chin. My last wish is that you provide her with a loving home and care for her in my stead."

The next photo slid onto the screen, a close-up showing Summer laughing at the camera as she clutched another teddy bear, this time a black one with a big red bow, her round cheeks glowing. She moved up close to the camera. Close enough to see every feature on her tiny face. The smile was so endearing, the little girl so happy and carefree. This beautiful child was innocent and would pay the price if he denied her.

"She is your daughter and you are her father. Please love her with all your heart as I have. Please," Deidre pleaded.

Carolyn pulled her hand away. "You believe her, don't you," she said, her voice shaking.

Disbelief shook him. What if this little girl was his daughter? What would he do if she were? Even the thought, the possibility of a child opened something inside him, something he'd never really felt before. He looked at Carolyn, saw her anguish and put his arm around her shoulders.

Carolyn pushed him away.

"We are going to have the DNA test redone. We'll pick a lab back in Boston and I will pay whatever it takes to have the testing done as fast as possible. We won't jump to any conclusions until then." He cleared his throat. "This is so difficult for you, finding out that I had relations with Deidre. I've hurt you in ways I never intended. ..ever. But we'll work this out, somehow. You'll see."

Carolyn wrapped her arms around her waist and nodded at the screen. "Lucas, look at her. She is so much like you... How could you think this isn't your child?" she asked, her voice breaking as she huddled in the corner of her chair.

"Carolyn, please, let's wait and see." As the video ended, despite his denials, he knew Summer was his daughter. He knew because the close-up shot revealed that Summer's left eye held the same tiny glint of a different color, the same as his mother's. It was a bit of pale yellow in the blue of the iris. A family trait. "Let's get that lawyer in here and then we can arrange the testing. After that, we'll go home and wait for the results."

He rose, waiting for his wife to stand, resisting the urge to take her in his arms and convince her that what had happened five years ago had been long over, even before it began. "I love you. My relationship with Deidre was wrong and a complete betrayal of you and of us. Whatever the tests show, I want you to know that I have never loved anyone the way I love you."

Slowly Carolyn stood, being careful to stay away from him. Regardless of what he wanted, he knew she would not allow him to touch her. "My only hope is that you see your way clear to forgive me," he said.

Without looking at him, she said, "Lucas, I can't talk to you about this, right now. I saw what I saw in the video."

CHAPTER FOUR

Days later, Carolyn placed a seafood casserole in the oven and set the timer. Her words in the lawyer's office had proven prophetic, because everything about her life had changed. The drive home had been a long, silent one with each mile forcing her to face the cold truth. She could think of little else but what Lucas had done with that woman who claimed that her child was his.

The easy closeness Carolyn and Lucas had shared disappeared as if it never existed. She'd moved into the guest bedroom, too tired to sleep as her mind went over that day at the Parker House Inn, and the phone call that had broken her heart.

Meanwhile, Lucas worked long hours, as he always did. Because of his behavior, Carolyn couldn't help but worry that maybe Deidre wasn't the only affair he'd had, that he might have spent the past few nights in the arms of another woman. She was embarrassed at how naive and foolish she'd been to never question anything her husband had told her. Just yesterday she'd considered hiring a private detective to follow him, something she was deeply ashamed of, but she'd found herself doing all sorts of things she would never have dreamed of a month ago.

She'd given everything, every part of herself, to her marriage. She'd never once considered having an affair, and she despised the fact that her husband had felt the need to have one. Sure, it had been rough going through the tests, trying to have a baby. But he wasn't the only one wishing that it would be over while praying for a baby to make their life together complete.

Trying to find a way to live while waiting for the test results, she'd invited their friends, Celia and Dave for dinner. As though everything was fine. It was better than facing the evening alone, which was what she'd been doing since seeing the video of Summer.

Lucas came up behind her and put his hands on her waist, something that had always made her lean back into his embrace. "Carolyn, I've finished setting the table. Anything else I can do?" he whispered close to her ear, sending tiny points of excitement hurtling down her body. She resisted the urge to lean into him and, instead, ran hot water into the sink in preparation for cleaning the frying pan and spatulas she'd used.

He continued to hold her gently. And she found herself powerless to resist him. "Carolyn, I know how hard this has been for you, this waiting and wondering."

She turned in his arms and gazed into his eyes, his body's warmth drawing her closer. "If you really know how difficult this is for me, why haven't you stayed home with me during the evening? It's lonely here with no one to talk to about all this."

He bowed his head, his forehead touching hers. "I wish I had. Most of the time I sat in my office trying to face the truth about me, about what I'd done, how stupid I've been. Wherever my thoughts took me, one thing remained the same. This is my fault. I hurt you. I'm sorry. So sorry for what I did. I can't say it enough."

She wanted to resist him, make him pay for what he did to her, to them. But she needed his arms around her, needed to feel his body pressed into hers. She missed him so much, his lovemaking, his caring touch, the feeling that they would always be together. She put her arms around his neck and raised her face to his.

He sighed, his lips touching hers, demanding and hot. She angled her body closer, feeling his erection against her tummy and writhing against it.

"Oh, Carolyn," he whispered against her mouth, his breath hot on her lips.

"Lucas," she whispered, pulling him closer, her need for him sweeping all other thoughts from her mind.

He picked her up. "We've got time," he said, holding her tight as they started for the bedroom.

"You're going to carry me upstairs?" she said, surprised. "You haven't done that in years."

"I may spend my days behind a desk but I can still carry my wife upstairs," he said, his embrace firm as he maneuvered through the living room toward the stairs just as the phone rang.

A mechanical voice blared from the phone on the hall table. "Call from Knowles Attorney at Law. Call from Knowles Attorney at Law."

He stopped. She slid from his arms. They stared at each other.

"You'd better take it," Carolyn said, her voice strained, her heart doing a slow, hard pound in her chest. She watched her husband's face as he spoke with the lawyer, his eyes on hers as he listened.

"I understand. So, it's conclusive." He fidgeted with the

handheld unit, shifting his weight from one foot to the other, his eyes swerving around the room. "Thanks. Yes. Please fax the results to my office as soon as you can." He hung up, coming toward her, pulling her into his arms, his body pressed to hers. "The test results prove that Summer is my daughter. I can't believe this. I have a daughter... How could I have a daughter?"

A chill ran down Carolyn's spine. He said the words with a reverence she hadn't heard from him before. "You have a daughter."

"I can't believe it," he said again, as if he hadn't heard her, his eyes shining with unshed tears. "But deep down, I knew by the spot of color in her left eye. I saw it. Mom had the same spot, the same yellow area in her iris."

Carolyn stepped out of his arms. "You were sure the day we saw the video, but you didn't tell me. You let me hope that there might be a chance that the DNA test was wrong. How could you?" she demanded.

He glanced at her, his expression gentle. "I wanted to protect you as long as I could. But, yes, I knew that Summer was my daughter. I don't know how it could have happened, but it did."

"How can you stand there and tell me you don't know how it happened! All these nights, you haven't been sitting in your office worried about me. You've been thinking about your daughter. Meanwhile, I've been home alone trying to make sense of things."

"I've been trying to figure out how it happened," he said.

"Oh, for heaven's sake, Lucas. You made this happen by having sex with this woman. How can you stand there and pretend this was fate when you broke our marriage vows?" Carolyn demanded, so angry she could barely breathe. "Stop lying to yourself," she said as she stomped upstairs.

She turned at the top of the stairs to face him as he stood

at the bottom looking up at her. "You had your fling and now you have your child. Congratulations."

With that she went into the guest bedroom and slammed the door. Throwing herself on the bed she cried until there were no tears left.

The next morning, Carolyn awoke to the sound of the phone ringing, once again the stupid, mechanical voice announcing the caller, only this time, it was her friend Celia's name. Carolyn didn't have a clue whether they'd shown up last night or not. She hadn't been able to hear anything over her tears.

She heard Lucas's voice, his consoling tone and his offer to have her call Celia back when she got up. But she wasn't getting up for a very long time. The man she'd thought she knew didn't exist anymore. And instead, she was faced with the fact that her husband was completely absorbed with his present circumstances, leaving her to work out her feelings toward him alone, to cope with the loss of her dream all over again.

She heard Lucas come up the stairs and scrambled to bury herself under the covers. When the door opened she called out, "What do you want?"

He entered the room, standing next to the door. "We need to talk, Carolyn."

"You're the one with the secrets. Why don't you start?" she asked sarcastically. She was done trying to be the perfect, caring wife.

"Last night was difficult for you, and I'm sorry."

She wanted to stay buried beneath the duvet, but if he was going to stand there talking, she decided to face him, to not back down or allow any feelings she had left for him sway her.

She sat up, bracing herself against the mound of pillows. "Lucas, if you'd behaved like my husband and not some philandering shell of a man, you wouldn't have to apologize. You have singlehandedly destroyed our marriage. I hope you're proud of what you've done."

She saw the hurt in his eyes, the way his hands shook as he held them against his face. "That was mean of me, but you deserved it," she said, swinging her feet over the side of the bed while hugging the duvet close to her body, realizing, as she looked at her feet, that she was still dressed in the clothes she'd worn yesterday.

"You're right. But we have to talk. I called the lawyer this morning, and he wants to know if we're going to be in Concord sometime this week to settle the estate."

"What do you want me to do about it? She's your daughter. And her mother was your lover," she said.

"She's *our* daughter, and she's going to be part of our lives. I want to talk this over with you. I need to have your support on this."

"My support?" She gawked. "You think after everything you've done that you're entitled to my support?"

"You're my wife, and you will be Summer's mother."

"Lucas! Wake up! I am not Summer's mother and I'm not your wife. You made sure of that." She couldn't look at the sorrowful expression on his face any longer. Instead, she focused on the embroidered edge of the duvet.

"Carolyn, Summer is my daughter. I can't abandon her now that her mother is gone."

"And you're not being fair. How long have I waited to have a baby, to share every bit of the experience with you? And now there's this...this child, who will remind me every single day of my life that my husband has been unfaithful, and I'm supposed to be her mother?"

Carolyn balled her hands into fists. "You should have been honest with me. About the affair and about this child. You knew the truth when we were at the lawyer's office.

And again you didn't respect me enough to tell me the truth."

Lucas rushed to the side of the bed and knelt in front of her. "I should have. I know that. And I have no explanation other than my own stupidity, my need to protect you. But now there is a child in our lives who just lost her mother and who will be going through a terrible time. I can't leave her to deal with that without me. I can't."

His eyes implored her to understand. "I realize that this is a lot for you to take in, but Summer needs me...needs us." He took her hand in his, his fingers gently stroking the soft skin of her wrist. "I can't imagine what life will be like for Summer now that her mother is gone. She's only four and she is going to be alone if we don't help her."

"Why do you keep saying we?" Carolyn asked, feeling her throat tighten.

"Carolyn, you're the most loving and kind person on the planet. And there is a little girl in need of everything you have to offer. Don't pass up the chance to help her because of the mistakes I made. Don't make her life more miserable because of something I did. I will do anything you ask if you will come to Concord with me."

Carolyn looked into his eyes and saw the truth of his words. He wanted to go to his daughter, and she wanted him to go. Despite her hurt and her fear of how this child would change their lives, she wanted him to go to his little girl. She wanted the little girl to have all the support and understanding possible. But Carolyn could not go there with him. Couldn't act as if nothing had happened, as if her life hadn't been tossed in the garbage by the man who claimed to love her.

"Why do you need me? There must be other people to help out. People she already knows. People who love her. What about Deidre's friends?"

"I don't know who Deidre's friends are, but the only way I can find out is to go back to Concord."

Lucas sighed deeply. "I promise you, Carolyn, that if you go with me, I will do whatever you ask where we are concerned. I will respect any decision you make once you've seen Summer. It's clear we need time to work on our problems. I won't deny that. But I also want you to see this little girl."

"Why are you so fixated on this, Lucas? A few days won't matter. You're a complete stranger to this child, and she's just lost her mother. What if you upset her? What good will that do?"

"I hope that doesn't happen, but if it does, I'll find a way to deal with it," Lucas said.

And then it dawned on her. Lucas didn't get how painful this was for her, or else he was driven only by what he wanted. He should have had some idea about how painful it would be for her to face the child he'd conceived with another woman. But he didn't.

And now he had a whole new focus in his life. He had a daughter, and his eagerness to see her made Carolyn feel invisible...unimportant.

Yet deep down, a part of her longed to see this child, a little girl who, through no fault of her own, had been thrust into their lives. What would it be like if, somehow, they could work things out between them and Lucas took over his little girl's life? How would holidays, like Christmas or Easter, be if Summer was with them? It was so easy to imagine those moments, moments Carolyn had already dreamed of, lived for all these years.

But she had to face the fact; regardless of how this little girl had come into their lives, she would become a part of their lives. If they could resolve their differences. How could she mother another woman's child when that child would trigger suspicions about her husband's behavior? Carolyn would always wonder what Lucas was doing, what he was really feeling, whenever she looked at the child he'd had with someone else. Carolyn had been living that way these past few weeks, and it had been awful. How could she continue, if they didn't spend time talking about all this? "Lucas, if we are going together to see Summer, I need you to tell me that that you aren't hiding anything more from me."

He nodded his head vigorously, his face tight with anxiety.

"Are you sure you're telling me everything about your relationship with Deidre? How am I to believe that you weren't in touch with her these past four years? Because it just doesn't make sense to me. What woman would spend the money to prove who the father of her child was without ever telling him about it?"

"I agree with you. I have no idea why Deidre did what she did. But I swear to you, I had no contact with her."

"And you and Deidre haven't been seeing each other?"

"Carolyn, I have not seen Deidre since those two days five years ago. I've done a lot of things wrong, but I want to get this right. What I said last night about Summer being my child is true. But you're my wife. I love you. And this is our child. I can't help but believe that your faith in God had something to do with this child entering our lives."

"What? You think this is some sort of divine intervention?"

"It's possible After all, we love each other. We've tried everything to have a baby. And I'm really sorry that Deidre died, she was essentially a good person. But her passing has given us the gift we've been dreaming of for years. It may not have happened in quite the way either of us wanted, but it is a chance for us to start our family."

She had always been a practicing Christian. She believed

in God's will and his plan for her and her life. Could it be that Lucas was right?

Was this how God worked in their lives? She wasn't sure. "Do you think it's possible?"

He nodded. "I do."

Seeing the anguish on his face, Carolyn clasped his hand, her love for him reawaking within her. This was a very difficult situation, and they would be a long time working through it, but if they could... She leaned across the bed to touch him, forcing back her fears.

If they were going to make their marriage work once again, she had to accept what had happened. If, in the end, they couldn't work things out, she had to be certain that she'd done what she could to save her marriage. "I'll go with you to see Summer."

He kissed her hand, a long sigh escaping his lips. "Thank you. You will not regret this. I promise you."

CHAPTER FIVE

They packed a few things and started out of town just as the sun began to warm the air. Carolyn couldn't help but feel anxious. As much as she wanted to support Lucas and Summer, she was still in shock over what had occurred in such a short time. Doubt continued to circle her thoughts, leaving her confused. Did she believe this might be God's will?

She felt suspended, dislocated, since the lawyer had called. The news that Lucas would now be responsible for his daughter didn't seem to be real, despite her earlier hope. "How are we going to make this all work?" she asked.

"To be honest, I'm still trying to figure out why Deidre didn't tell me."

"Maybe she never intended that you find out."

"But why?"

"Who knows. I don't," Carolyn said, feeling uneasy.

He glanced over at her. "I mean that she seemed so straight forward about things. I'm surprised she didn't contact me, that's all."

"Maybe her cheating wasn't just with another woman's

husband," Carolyn said. "Maybe she didn't tell anyone the truth."

"I hadn't thought of that, but I really didn't know her." Searching for something that would help to keep her mind from twisting and turning, to keep her worried thoughts away from meeting this child, she said, "Did you make a reservation for us for tonight?"

"No. I didn't think of it. But we can do that easily when we get there."

Lucas drove carefully through the city streets toward the highway leading out of town. "Carolyn, I have been so busy building up my company, making plans for us, for when we have a family, that I didn't take in what it would really mean to have a child in our lives. But now that this little girl is here with us, it's as if we're being given a chance to have what we always dreamed of. I want to be there for her."

"It's just that there is so much to think about, about our lives, the changes."

He squeezed her hand a little tighter. "We'll figure it all out together. We'll see how Summer is doing when we get to the house. The nanny will be there and probably a couple of Deidre's closest friends."

"You know where Deidre lives... I mean, lived?" Carolyn asked, wondering how he would have known if he hadn't seen her since the end of the affair over five years ago.

"Mr. Knowles told me she lived in the same house as when I knew her."

Reality crashed down on Carolyn, billowing around her like an unwanted mist. Memories of those lonely nights when she'd waited for Lucas to come home, to make love to her, praying that this time there would be a baby for them. Believing his absence meant he was building a future for their family.

She believed in marriage, had been raised in a home

where vows of any kind were taken seriously, and none more than the marriage vow. She wanted to take him back and put her whole heart into forgetting the past. They had married right out of college and had had their share of disagreements like any couple, but never something like this.

There were so many questions and so few answers. Why had Deidre chosen not to tell Lucas about Summer when she was alive? Wouldn't she have wanted her daughter to be close to her dad and his family?

Carolyn couldn't imagine any woman who would have behaved that way. She certainly wouldn't have. She would have insisted that the child's father share in the responsibility for caring for and raising it. She would want her daughter to have all the love and support possible, regardless of how she felt about the father. So how could Deidre not be in touch with Lucas and still expect him to step in as parent? None of this made any sense...

"Carolyn, honey, time to wake up," Lucas said softly.

"What?" she asked, suddenly realizing she'd drifted off. After not sleeping for days, the smooth motion of the car had lulled her to sleep. Sitting up straight, she glanced out the window at the quiet boulevard basking in the midmorning sun. "Should I put Deidre's address into the GPS?"

"No. We're only a few minutes away from her house."

It was humiliating to realize that her husband had been to Deidre's home. Had they made love in her bedroom? Carolyn's stomach sank, pressing into her backbone. Of course they had. They wouldn't have needed to hide out in a hotel room to carry on their affair when Deidre's home was available and waiting.

Carolyn closed her eyes, trying to resist the image of her husband and Deidre making love in the home she was about to enter. A sharp ache close to her heart made her grit her teeth. She couldn't wait to get away from the place. "I'm dreading this."

"I am in a way, too. I'm worried about how she'll react to us appearing in her life right now..." He turned right onto a tree-lined street, weaving through the many twists and turns of a roadway designed to slow traffic around homes whose gabled entrances, brick exteriors and long, elegant windows spoke of wealth and prestige.

Carolyn shrank into the seat, suddenly wishing she hadn't come with Lucas. She didn't want to see this house, this place where her husband had made love to another woman. The car slowed as Lucas pulled into a driveway surrounded by a hedge that protected the house from the street, the massive gardens sweeping toward the entrance, flashing bright red and yellow flowers of all sizes and shapes. Following the curve of the driveway, they stopped in front of a massive dark wood door.

Lucas turned off the engine. "How are you doing?" he asked, turning to her his eyes filled with concern. "I realize that this isn't easy for you," he murmured, taking her hand in his. "If you'd rather, I can go in first, if it would make it easier for you..."

Her heart hammered against her rib cage. Could she go in there? Could she face a little girl who was about to be part of their life?

She glanced around, hoping to see other vehicles along the circular drive. There weren't any. It had been several weeks since Deidre's passing, and yet Carolyn had expected to see evidence that people were still coming to check on a little girl who had lost her mommy. Where were all this woman's friends? Or didn't she have any?

"I'm not sure I can do this. Go into the house where you slept with another woman."

"It's all right if you can't. You've come this far with me, more than I expected or deserved."

"Maybe the nanny isn't home. Maybe she took Summer to friends' or to the library," Carolyn said, the knot in her stomach hardening.

Without a word, Lucas came around to her door, opened it and took her hand in that reassuring way of his. Suddenly she felt faint. "I'm not sure I can do this, Lucas."

He squeezed her fingers. "You can. I'm right here if you need me." He took her hand and led her to the imposing front door, his fingers pressing the doorbell as his eyes held hers. "This will all be okay. I promise you. We'll be okay."

The door opened and a tall woman with dark hair and penetrating brown eyes greeted them. "You must be Lucas Turner. Come in," she offered, leading the way into the formal living room to the right of the entrance hall.

"I am, and this is my wife, Carolyn," Lucas said, his arm coming around Carolyn's shoulders.

The woman's expression was one of kindness. "I'm Summer's nanny, Lisa Gomez. I've cared for Summer since she was born."

She pointed to the sofa opposite the fireplace. "I'm aware of Deidre's intentions concerning Summer, and I want you to know I approve of them. A child should be with her father in a situation like this. Summer has a lovely photo of you, Mr. Turner."

Carolyn sat on the edge of the sofa her mind reeling. A photo of Lucas? She turned to Lisa. "You have a photo of my husband. Why?"

Lisa glanced quizzically at Lucas before she answered. "He is Summer's father. Deidre wanted Summer to be able to recognize her father. Deidre's company worked closely with his company, and I'm sure they stayed in touch through work, although she never said as much."

Lisa raised her eyebrows, her gaze resting on Carolyn's face, a look of understanding dawning on her face. "I'm terribly sorry, Mrs. Turner. I don't know why, but I thought Lucas was single when he and Deidre met..."

Lucas had sworn he hadn't been involved in Deidre's business after the affair. He'd claimed Brad looked after anything Deidre's company needed. Was that the truth? Had her husband been here since that weekend? Was she the only one who didn't know what was going on? Had Brad and Lucas both hidden the truth from her? Lucas wouldn't do that, of that she was certain.

Tears burned her eyes. She fought to regain her equilibrium, deciding to say nothing more to this woman. Her hands clammy, her breath coming in short gasps, she asked, "Could I see the photo of my husband?"

"That's not necessary," Lucas said.

"I'd like to see the photo of my husband," she said, suspicion writhing through her at Lucas's objection.

Lisa left the room and came back a few minutes later, holding the framed photo out to Carolyn. "Deidre wanted Summer to understand that she had a dad who didn't live with them and what he looked like."

Carolyn searched the photo for clues as to where it had been taken...a park somewhere. She didn't recognize the photo or the place, but the smile on Lucas's face was playful and open. How could he have been looking that way if their relationship was a quick hookup, a fling, as he'd described it? And why had they been in a park she didn't recognize? "I thought you had no role in Summer's life, that you knew nothing about her until the lawyer called," she said.

"I swear to you I didn't," Lucas said, his smile forced as he glanced across at Lisa. "You've never met me before, have you, Ms. Gomez?"

"That's correct. I knew you by the photo only. But I

assumed she was in touch with you over her arrangements, Mr. Turner," Lisa said, a small frown forming.

Lucas shook his head emphatically.

"Where was this photo taken?" Carolyn asked.

Lucas stared at the picture. "She must have photoshopped it. I've never been in a park with Deidre."

"After her dad passed away last March, Deidre decided that, since there really weren't any close family connections, she wanted to provide Summer with a sense of belonging," Lisa said, her gaze one of disbelief as she continued to stare at Lucas. "Once Deidre made a decision, she stuck to it. Because of that, I assumed you knew about Summer and that one day you would show up here. Deidre didn't say that, exactly, but I am pretty sure she intended to find you and encourage you to be involved in Summer's life."

Lucas clutched Carolyn's hand. "I never heard one word from Deidre after that weekend. I swear to you, I didn't know any of this."

"Then tell me why she made all those plans. It doesn't make sense to me, and it clearly doesn't make sense to Lisa, the woman who was closest to the situation."

"Carolyn, I'm telling you, I am as much in the dark as you are."

"Lucas, please don't lie to me. Did she ever try to contact you about Summer before this?" Carolyn asked, her quiet tone belying her inner anger.

"I wasn't in touch with Deidre after those two days. I had no reason to go near her. I knew it was a mistake, and I wanted to get away from all of it as fast as possible."

Carolyn felt hot tears on her cheeks and was mortified that a stranger was able to witness her pain, her embarrassment She looked her husband over carefully, searching his expression for any indication he was not telling her the truth. "And you never once came to see Deidre or Summer?"

"I swear to you, Carolyn. I didn't know about any of this."

"Mrs. Turner, I only want what is best for Summer. But I realize the two of you might need a chance to talk this over. The accident and its aftermath was a shock for everyone. I have to go now to pick up Summer from kindergarten. If you'd like, I can take her to the playground on the way home, give you both a little time to talk this out." Lisa glanced from one to the other.

"Yes, please do that." Lucas cleared his throat. "Then bring Summer home. We'd like to meet her."

Carolyn watched warily as Lisa left the house. Everything felt surreal, out of place. Fighting her fear, she turned to her husband, praying for him to say the words that would make everything in her life right again.

CHAPTER SIX

Exhaustion burned behind Lucas's eyes. It had been a difficult drive here, and even though he knew he would have to explain so many things to Carolyn, he hadn't expected her to be so suspicious. She had to know he was telling the truth. He'd always told her the truth, shared everything with her until his involvement with Deidre. Shame had forced him to hide what he did. Shame and the belief that nothing would come of the two days he'd spent with Deidre. That his secret would never harm the one woman he loved.

He reached out for Carolyn's hand, entwining his fingers with hers. "I don't know anything about the photo or Deidre's plans."

"I don't know what to believe. This is really difficult and awful for me," Carolyn said, pulling her hand away.

The loss of her touch chilled him to his core. "We will find a way through all of this. But first we need to think about Summer. She needs us. We need to work out how we will manage and how we will take Summer home with us." As much as he wanted to, he didn't touch Carolyn. He knew she wouldn't want him to. "Carolyn, I know we can work this out, like before when we had problems," he pleaded, his stomach aching with dread.

She moved away from him, confusion clear in her eyes. "How can we? Deidre chose you to be the custodial parent for Summer, even though she didn't discuss it with you beforehand. But Summer represents your lies and the way you broke your vows. Lucas, there are two of us in this marriage. We are not supposed to have secrets, hidden lives."

"We don't!"

"That's what you want me to believe," she said, and Lucas couldn't miss the harsh tone in her voice, so unlike his wife.

Feeling at a complete loss as to what to say or do, he slumped in the chair. "How can I convince you that I had nothing to do with Deidre these past five years?"

She stared around the room as if looking for a chance to leave. "I wish there was a way you could convince me, but it will take time."

"Yes, we need time. But there are other considerations. There's a child who will be here soon, who has no idea why you and I are in her home."

"I'm not responsible for what happened here, and I'm not responsible for your daughter. You are, and you have to do whatever you need to do," Carolyn said, her voice low and controlled, her eyes dark pools in stark contrast to her pale skin.

"Carolyn, I don't want to do this without you. You're my wife and I love you. I have to figure out how to handle this. I have to find a way to be a father to Summer when I don't even know her. We will have to decide how we should live, whether she comes home with us right now, or I stay here for a while to see what arrangements need to be made about Deidre's estate, the dissolution of assets and what I'm expected to do."

He rubbed his hands together slowly, as his mind worked

through the possible issues surrounding Deidre's death and estate, and all the while his thoughts were with Summer, of what the next few hours and days would be like for his daughter. "I've never been a parent. I don't know how to do this. Having a child was always just an idea to me."

"But now it's real, with real decisions to be made," Carolyn said.

"I hear you. But I don't know what to do. We're in an emergency situation and have a lot to think about in a very short time. I need your help."

Carolyn stood, her hands clenched at her sides as she stared at him. "Did you hear yourself? Did you hear how selfish you sound?"

"What? I'm trying to figure out what to do. I can't do that without your help, Carolyn."

"You never once talked about me, about how I feel, about what this will do to our lives together. All you can think about is doing what Deidre wants. She's dead. She's not coming back. And yet you didn't, for one minute, stop and consider what I'm going through, did you? All you want from me is my help. You want me to make this better for you."

She scraped her hair off her face and blotted her cheeks with her fingers, her voice shaking. "I'm just as important in this situation as you are, as Summer is. You need to consider my feelings, talk things out with me. But instead of that, you go on and on about what *you're* going to do."

He stared at her face, at the anger in her eyes. How had he gotten this so wrong? "Carolyn, I didn't mean it that way. I'm so used to assessing a situation and deciding the best course of action to solve the problem. It's how I think."

Carolyn picked up her purse and slung it over her shoulder. "This is not a situation, Lucas. This is real life, where people you claim to love are hurting and sad. Summer is going to miss her mother for a very long time. You are not going to have your lovely well-ordered life where every problem has a solution anymore. You will have to face each issue with your daughter with your heart, not your head. But most of all, I will not have you making decisions without me having a say in how we do things. This is my life, my marriage, and I will no longer be told what decision you've made and simply go along with it."

He hadn't seen his wife this upset in a long time. "I'm as concerned and worried about all this as you are. I deal with it differently, mostly by focusing on what can be done, but that in no way means I don't want your input on this."

"You don't get it, do you?"

"Get what?" he asked, confused and really, really scared.

"You and I need to go home and talk this over between the two of us before we make a decision that will change our lives forever. Lisa is clearly concerned for Summer. She will look after her as long as needed. A few weeks won't make any difference. There's no rush to sell the house. Summer may need to be left in her kindergarten to give her a chance to get over the loss of her mother before she faces any other changes."

"Children adapt," he said defensively.

"I'm sure she will, given time, love and caring. Meanwhile, if this is to work out for everyone involved, we need to go home, talk this all over and decide how we will cope with having a child."

"Is that how you see this, as something done to us? It may have been, but we're the adults here. We understand what's at stake." How could Carolyn even consider leaving a little girl who had just lost her mother? This wasn't like her, not at all. "Carolyn, I can't leave Summer here without her family. We are her family now. I can't do it, and neither can you. You love children. And this little girl lost her mother. We may have to move in here for a while, but in the end, she will be coming home with us."

"You're not listening to me. This is too fast, way too fast. We need time to work this out. We both do if we are to stay together. It's too much too soon. I need to..." She eased away from him. "I can't stay here and watch you decide things based on what you want. There are three of us in this, three people's feelings to consider. Ignoring what I want, my opinion and ideas, isn't right. Life doesn't work that way, Lucas."

"But I want you to be with me when I meet her." Was she suggesting that they simply walk away? Where had all of this gone so wrong? "When we got in the car this morning, I never imagined that we'd be coming here only to leave again."

"And you didn't share that with me, did you?" Carolyn said.

"I didn't and that was wrong. But none of this is easy for either of us," he protested.

"You and I should have talked this over, thought this through. I can't be part of this until we do."

"You can't really want me to walk away, can you? It's just that right now you're hurt and upset. You'll feel differently when you see Summer."

She focused her gaze on him. "Okay. Before she gets back here let's run through the possibilities."

"Which are?" he asked, suddenly aware that he had never considered that there might be a different answer than the one he'd figured out.

"Summer's a little girl who has only known the life she's living right now. How can we assume that moving her to our place, taking her away from everything that is familiar is going to make her life better? What if she has family here who could take her? An aunt and uncle, maybe? I have to believe that Deidre chose you because she believed you'd do what was best for her daughter. And that's what you and I have to consider. Have you considered that if we decide not to take her, there will have to be other options for her care?"

Shock sparked through him. "Carolyn, not for a minute have I considered not taking her. I thought you understood that. We've waited all our married lives for a chance to have children. Now we have that chance."

Carolyn closed her eyes for a few moments, her body trembling. "Lucas, there is more than one answer here. There has to be. I'm not ready to take on the care of that little girl so soon. There has to be a way to work this out so that we have time to adjust to what all of this means." She looked straight at him, her expression one of determination. "If you're not willing to do that, I have no other option but to leave you here to work things out on your own."

"Leave? You can't. I mean you wouldn't leave a child who needed you." He struggled to accept her words. "Carolyn, I'll make a reservation for us at a hotel where we can stay while we work out how to do this. If you like, we'll wait to meet Summer later. I'll leave a note for Lisa, and that way she'll know how to find us. I'm sure that if you think about this, you'll come to realize that being with us in our home is the best answer for Summer."

"Please, Lucas, I can't do this right now. I need time to come to grips with what has happened to you and to me, to our marriage. Yes, Summer's care is important, but she is in the right place, at least for now. I will not make a snap decision about something that will affect the rest of my life. If you won't try to understand how much I need time to think about this, I'm going home." She looked into his eyes, holding his gaze. "I want you to come with me, but that's up to you."

"Carolyn, please don't."

"Lucas," she whispered, her voice thick. "It's better this

59

way. I don't want to fight with you, but I can't decide to take custody of this child this quickly."

By her resolute expression, he knew she meant it. "Carolyn, I wish you'd stay. We could get to know Summer a little, see how much she needs us to care for her, to give her love and stability in her life," he said, making one last attempt to convince her.

"I wish I could, too. But I can't do this, not this way." She held out her hands for the car keys. "I'm sure you can rent a vehicle if you need one."

He watched her walk toward the door, his heart pounding in his chest, his eyes filling with tears. Loss cascaded over him as he followed her, wanting to reach out to her one last time.

As Carolyn opened the door, she turned to him, her eyes meeting his. "I guess it's too late to ask you to see things my way."

He swallowed, feeling haggard and worn out. His gaze shifted from hers while his jumbled thoughts sought a response that would make Carolyn stay.

Yet it was clear from the expression on her face that Carolyn's mind was made up. He touched her shoulder, wanting to pull her into his arms, but knew the warning signs, the stiff set of her shoulders, the fingers clenched on the strap of her purse. Carolyn would not allow him to embrace her. "I don't want you to leave, but I understand you have to. You have a safe drive, and call me when you get home, will you?" he asked, feeling awkward and out of place.

"Of course." She fumbled with strap of her purse, not looking at him. Without another word, she left the house.

CHAPTER SEVEN

Her hands shaking Carolyn struggled to put her home address into the GPS. She had no idea how to get out of the city to the highway. Her only clear idea was that she had to get away from here, away from the pain and agony, the disappointment and fear.

She wanted Lucas to come running out the door, get into the car with her and agree to leave for home with her. She might have been willing to meet Summer, to stay overnight and drive home tomorrow while they talked. But none of that was possible given Lucas's attitude.

Her destination finally loaded into the GPS, she eased out of the driveway, her eyes searching the windows of Deidre's house for any sign of her husband. There was none. He had decided to remain inside the house, not even coming out to the car to make sure she was okay to drive.

Gripping the wheel, she started down the driveway, her head aching, tears streaming down her cheeks.

Concentrate. You can't make it home if you don't.

Maybe she should check into a hotel and wait until tomorrow to leave. It would be easier, and by morning, she might be able to get Lucas to see reason. Her heart lifted at the idea, then came crashing down. Their last few moments together had proven that her influence over her husband paled in the face of his concern for his newly-discovered daughter.

Besides, she couldn't fight with him any longer. She needed to get home, to talk to her brother. Brad would be able to offer suggestions about what to do, how to get Lucas to see the truth. Their marriage had been through enough between the stress of fertility testing and Lucas's confession of his affair. To think that he was suddenly willing to risk the fragile remains of their relationship in order to raise another woman's child, a child he claimed he wasn't involved with, hurt her to the core.

As she listened to the soothing female voice directing her through town to the highway she had a horrible sinking feeling that this would not turn out well, not because Lucas didn't want to fix it but because she didn't know if she could go through more loss.

Their inability to conceive a child had been so devastating. But facing the cruel truth that Lucas could father a child meant it was her fault. She was inadequate; she had been the cause of their unhappiness all along. All these years, all the times they'd tried for a baby, she'd been the reason they couldn't have a family. A sob shook her.

Focus. Focus on the moment.

As she reached the highway, she instructed the phone to dial her brother's number and he answered on the first ring. "Where are you? I called the house to talk to Lucas when he didn't show at work. What's going on?"

"I'm on my way home from Concord," she said, feeling relieved at the sound of her brother's voice.

"What? Why were you in Concord? Where's Lucas? I need to talk to him."

She did her best to remain calm while she told Lucas what had happened and about the DNA results.

"You're kidding me! I had no idea that he'd had an affair...and now a child? What in hell is going on with Lucas?" Brad asked.

Had Lucas not told Brad anything?

"You can see why I had to leave. He had an affair and now he's obsessed with the child from that relationship. All the times I tried to get him to understand how important a child was to me, how much I wanted to be a mother. And now this little girl is all that matters."

"Carolyn, you know that's not true. Lucas loves you. He always has. Sure, he made a mistake, and he is definitely making one now, but you need to give him a little time to sort things out. I'm sure once he has a chance to see what being responsible for this little girl means, he'll be back to you, begging you to help him figure out the best plan. I agree with you. It's too sudden."

Carolyn moved into the left lane, accelerating as she passed a transport truck. She was driving way too fast but she didn't care. She had to get home. "I'm not so sure. He's completely determined to bring Summer home with him, to be her daddy and provide her with a good home. He hasn't given me, or what I need, a thought since we arrived at Deidre's house. It's as if I don't exist. Brad, I'm afraid."

"Of what?"

"That Lucas has been involved in Summer's life all along. He denies it, but I can't believe him. And the photo the nanny had was so upsetting. Lucas said he didn't know about it, but I can't believe that he didn't. It was a photo taken in a park I didn't recognize. Someone had to have taken it, and by the smile on his face, it was someone he cared about. On top of that, the nanny said that Deidre wanted Summer to know what her father looked like. That's why the photo was there.

But what if it was more than that? Brad, I can't face this. I can't.

"Take it easy. Remember you're driving and it's not safe for you to be worrying and distracted behind the wheel."

She eased her foot off the accelerator. The blare of a horn sounded as the car behind her pulled out and passed her. "If he has hidden other things from me, my marriage is over. I might be able to forgive him for the affair, but if he's been seeing her and his child all this time, I can't forgive him for that."

"Sis, you're upset. But please just drive carefully and make it back here in one piece. I'll be waiting for you and we'll talk. Okay?" he said, his voice filled with concern and compassion.

"Okay." Talking to her brother made her feel a little better than she had when she left Lucas. But Brad made everyone feel safe, listened to everyone's woes and always seemed to have the right answer. When they were growing up, she had often sought his advice. "Thanks. What would I do without you? I'm so glad you were on the other end of the line when I called."

"Me, too. I'll be there when you get back. And call me if you need to. You hear?"

"I will. I promise." Just knowing Brad was waiting for her made the drive so much easier. She felt calm enough to concentrate on her driving as the road unwound in a long ribbonlike arc of asphalt.

Hours later, having listened to an audio book for the remainder of the trip, she pulled into her driveway, to the home she shared with Lucas. As she pressed the remote to open the garage door, she fought back loneliness so profound her breath felt trapped in her throat. For one fleeting moment, she doubted her decision to walk out on Lucas.

Maybe if she had stayed, encouraged him to talk about

how they would care for Summer together, put aside her hurt feelings, they could have made some decisions.

Lucas watched the car pull away and his heart turned over in his chest. He didn't want Carolyn to leave. He should have gone out and begged her to stay, but he hadn't because... because he didn't know what to say to her.

He'd felt this way so many times before when they'd been trying to have a baby. Carolyn had been so intent on getting pregnant that everything else in their lives was forgotten. They'd stopped talking about anything other than having a baby. Their time together had become charged with waiting to see if Carolyn had a positive pregnancy test.

When Carolyn had wanted to take Summer's custody slowly, to consider all the aspects of what it meant to take her, he'd been surprised. Having witnessed her obsession with having a baby, he'd assumed that Carolyn would be as willing as he was to take the little girl into their lives as soon as they possibly could.

His wife wanted a child, and Summer needed parents. To him it was a gift from God, the answer to their prayers.

Yet when Carolyn had protested, his first instinct had been to defend his position, his plan. He'd been hurt that Carolyn didn't seem to feel as he did about Summer. Yet he knew he needed Carolyn more now than he ever had in his entire life.

He'd screwed everything up. But one thing he was thankful for: he'd held his tongue. When she accused him of being selfish, he'd almost said something about her selfish obsession these past years. If he'd said that, there would be no chance that she would ever listen to him again.

But Carolyn had been right about one thing. They needed to talk this out together, and he had to take it easy, let her express her fear and reservations about assuming custody of Summer. He had a few reservations of his own, including how they would cope with a child who was old enough to realize that her mother was gone, but too young to understand why her life would have to change.

As he watched Carolyn drive away he wanted to run after her, tell her how much he loved her and that she was right. They needed to sort out their feelings and expectations before they could make a decision about Summer. And that meant they needed time alone together to prepare for their new life.

Yet he couldn't walk out on his daughter. She'd already faced long days and nights without her mother. It was so important that Summer have people around her who loved her while she learned to cope with her new circumstances.

His heart heavy, he watched out the window, seeing her brake lights glow red as Carolyn pulled out of the driveway. He knew his wife would call Brad to seek his advice. Brad would be angry, and rightfully so. Lucas doubted that Brad would understand his point of view, and he couldn't blame him.

Lucas glanced around the room, remembering the two nights he'd spent in this house when he and Deidre had been together. Deidre had used birth control, something she'd been very emphatic about. How had the birth control failed? Deidre had loved details, had reveled in getting everything right.

Another idea skirted the edge of his mind. He couldn't imagine someone like Deidre taking any chances with her personal life. Yet she had insisted that they work in her home, a home equipped with all the technology to do so. Had she intentionally misled him? Had she chosen him to be the father of her child, invited him into her home, intending to get pregnant, keep the child and continue on with her life?

Had her father's death made her realize that if she passed away, Summer would be alone? His mind ran over the possibilities as his eyes took in the space that appeared unchanged from five years ago.

Focused on his thoughts, he was about to head to the kitchen for a glass of water when the door from the garage opened. Lisa walked in carrying a pink Dora the Explorer backpack while Summer followed holding a huge brown bear, the one in the video. His heart soared as he looked at his daughter. She was even more beautiful than the photos he'd seen. Uncertain about how to approach the little girl staring at him, he smiled, trying to put her at ease.

Lisa put the backpack on the end of the kitchen counter. "Summer, do you know who this is?" she asked, her gaze sweeping from Lucas to Summer.

Summer promptly popped her thumb into her mouth and reached for Lisa's hand.

Lisa patted Summer's curls soothingly as she spoke. "Remember the man in the photograph? He's come to see you."

His chest tight, he knelt in front of his little girl and held out his arms. "Hi, Summer, I'm your dad," he said.

Summer stopped sucking her thumb and stared at him, her eyes filling with glossy tears. "No! Mommy. I want Mommy."

He edged closer. "I'm so sorry," he said softly. His little girl needed him, and he would be here for her. "Come, let me hold you," he whispered, marveling at how natural it felt to be here with his daughter.

"No! Mommy!" Summer screamed, her arms reaching for Lisa as tears flowed down her tiny face.

"Lucas, I'm sorry about this," Lisa said, picking her up and snuggling her close as Summer continued to sob, her face pressed into Lisa's chest.

Helpless to figure out what to say or do, Lucas watched in dread as Summer stared at him, her eyes dark with fear. He was a stranger to his only child, his daughter. She didn't want anything to do with him.

He hadn't expected this. He'd assumed that she would recognize him from the photo, remember what her mother had said, and would want him to hold her. He struggled to stem the flood of fear flooding through him. He was in over his head. He had no idea what he was doing or how to do it. He'd never considered that Summer would react this way. How would he ever manage to care for his daughter if she was afraid of him? He glanced at Lisa, seeking her support.

"Lucas, please don't worry. Summer has been very upset since...you know. She'll be better soon. You'll see."

He didn't see at all. He hadn't been around kids very much, and he had no idea how to deal with them. Now, with his daughter so upset, he didn't have a clue how to reach out to her. Yet he knew he had to if he was going to be her dad. Instinctively, he backed away, keeping the smile on his face, his heart heavy with disappointment. "Summer. Your daddy is going to wait in the living room. Is that okay?"

Summer, her face buried in Lisa's neck, didn't respond.

CHAPTER EIGHT

I t was so good to be home, but so awful to be going into the house she and Lucas shared knowing he wasn't here. As upset as she'd been leaving, facing the house alone somehow made the trouble between her and her husband a fact and, in a very clear way, horribly real to her.

Never in her wildest dreams had she ever imagined she'd be faced with her marriage in tatters, and suspicion and distrust toward the man she'd loved since high school. His infidelity changed everything she'd believed about her marriage and her husband.

If she needed any proof of how much her marriage was in trouble, she had only to look at what happened a few hours ago. The Lucas she knew would never have allowed her to leave, not without following her, if only to say goodbye and to reassure her that he would miss her. She was so accustomed to his presence in her life...

She grabbed her overnight bag from the backseat and started toward the door leading into the house. Just as she unlocked it, she heard her brother's truck pull into the driveway. Relief flooded her. She raced out to him. "I'm so glad to see you, Brad," she said, wrapping her arms around his neck and hugging him close.

"That husband of yours needs his butt kicked," he said, patting her shoulders as she clung to him. "I'm glad you got home safely."

"Me, too," she said, watching as he put her overnight bag on the floor by the cupboard and moved to the counter where he ran water and filled the coffeepot. Her brother familiar movements comforted her. He was the best brother anyone could wish for. Leaning against the counter as he moved about her kitchen, finding cups and getting cream out of the fridge, she relaxed a little. Whatever came next, her brother would be here for her.

"Sis, despite how dumb Lucas is behaving, it's going to be okay," he said, pouring two cups of coffee and passing one to her. "Things seem pretty awful right now, but you and Lucas have been through lots of stuff together. This won't be any different." He put cream and sugar in his cup and offered her both.

"Just cream for me," she said.

"You've given up sugar in your coffee?" he asked.

"Yeah. I saw a program on the ill effects of too much sugar and decided to cut back," she said distractedly as she placed her hands firmly around her cup, sipping slowly.

Lucas's gaze assessed her. "You've had a rotten time of it, haven't you?"

Her hands began to shake at his words. The cup clattered onto the counter, coffee spilling over the edge. "I don't know what to do."

"I'm so sorry, Sis," Lucas said, putting his hand on hers. "What can I do?"

"Help me understand what is going on."

"I'm still convinced that Lucas will come to his senses and realize what a total jerk he's been."

"But that doesn't change how awful I feel, how mixed up I am," Carolyn said as she edged onto one of the navy-blue leather stools at the kitchen island. She'd put so many hours of planning into this space when they were remodeling their home.

The off-white cabinetry had been suggested by the interior decorator and she'd loved the look of it. Lucas had insisted on an extra-large fridge with lots of freezer space so he could buy whatever amounts he needed for the meals he liked to cook. Unable to stop her eyes from moving from one beautiful part of her kitchen to the other, a flood of memories overtook her. "Remember the time Lucas cooked all those ribs for the staff, using both ovens? And the huge mess afterward?" she said.

"I do. He invited the whole office and did most of the work. It was a great party, and everyone appreciated being here."

"It wouldn't have been so messy if Lucas hadn't spilled a platter of ribs. I can still see the two of you trying to get the gooey, sticky juice stuff off the ceramic tiles," Carolyn said.

"You were a good sport about that. Most women would have thrown a hissy fit and called for a cleaning service."

"There are so many good memories here, Brad. But right now, I can't imagine how we're going to work out our problems. He brushed me off when I asked about this Deidre person. It's as though he thinks I'm simply overreacting and that I'll get over the affair and accept his way of doing things with Summer."

"Do you want me to talk to him? Get him to see what he's done?"

"I don't know what good that would do. I still can't figure how he's going to manage a little girl who has just lost her mother. He's never been a parent. He's never had to look after a child before. And what if he causes Summer serious emotional issues by forcing her to leave everything she is familiar with so soon after her mother's death? All to satisfy his need to be a parent."

"It's that serious, is it?" Brad asked, sitting on the stool next to her.

"Worse. He's not listening. It's as if he is trying to make up for something...not where I'm concerned, but something is weird with him."

Brad took her hand in his. "I cannot picture how it must have felt for him to find out he has a daughter. But Lucas's always been so cool under pressure, so able to manage everything. You said he spent most evenings after he found out about Summer in his office. Maybe he was trying, in Lucas fashion, to come to terms with what it meant to suddenly find that he's a father."

"Well, that's fine for him. But am I supposed to sit around and wait for him to come to me, to be the person who supports his decision?" she asked, feeling her throat tighten.

"Don't say that. Think back to the day you had the car accident. Remember? Instead of rushing in and staying by your side, he first arranged to have the surgeon meet him in emergency where he grilled him about how the procedure would be done."

She couldn't help but smile. "Yeah, he arrived in my room, the surgeon trailing behind him, the surgery time set. When he finally felt everything was under control, he sat at my bedside with the most anxious look in his eyes."

"See? You simply have to trust Lucas. He'll work this out." He patted her hand before getting up to freshen their coffees. Passing her mug to her, he said, "I realize that it doesn't help you deal with his betrayal, but right now you need to think about you. You've been through so much in such a short time. Why don't you just take a long, hot bath, read something? Get some rest. Give this a little time. Your husband tends to act first and seek other people's opinions later."

"But this is different. This is me. His wife. First, I find out he's had an affair and a child. Then I find out he hasn't got time for my feelings."

"Have you considered the possibility that this whole thing is as big an adjustment for him as it is for you?"

"Adjustment? He's anxious to take over with Summer. That hardly sounds like he's having trouble adjusting."

"Think about it. Lucas's an only child. He never had anyone in his life totally dependent on him until Summer. That has to cause him all kinds of anxiety regardless of how he appears to be behaving."

"Anything is possible, I suppose. It's just that I don't know where we go from here."

He came around the island and hugged her tight. "Sis, one of the major traits of our family to let our hurt feelings rule our thinking. I'm proof of that. Maria has helped me see how easily I can be hurt, then withdraw to lick my wounds. For my money, that's what you're doing now."

"You think I should go back to Concord?"

"I think you should do whatever it is that makes you happy. You and Lucas have been happy and will be again, but not until you work out your differences. Listen to Lucas. Find out what he's going through. I'm betting you're both going through a lot of the same stuff."

"But he's ready to jump into fatherhood without so much as a word of how it will work with Summer, a child he knows nothing about. He's so stubborn," she said.

"That's part of what you can help Lucas with. You understand what a huge change this is for Summer as well as for both of you." He touched her cheek. "You're not a quitter. Talk to Lucas again. Tell him how you really feel..."

He looked into her eyes and she saw how much her

brother cared. She wasn't in a strange city trying to cope with a little girl who had been traumatized. She really didn't understand what her husband was going through right now, and she never would if she didn't get in touch with him again. They had so many issues to work on, but none of it would matter if they couldn't talk to each other.

"Okay. I guess it wouldn't hurt for me to make the first move. I'll stay here tonight, then head back tomorrow morning."

"As a show of support, I'll take your car and gas it up before I head over to my condo. Maria is anxious to hear how you and Lucas are doing."

"That's so sweet. Visited any jewelry stores lately?" she teased, happy for her brother.

"I'm not telling you, Ms. Matchmaker," he said, laughing as he went out the back door.

She watched him leave, thankful she had a brother and aware of how much she depended on him for advice. Lucas didn't have the option of relying on a brother or sister. She would remember that the next time they talked.

Should she call him now? Her stomach clenched at the thought.

After an hour of indecision, Carolyn dialed Lucas's cell phone. He answered on the first ring. "I'm so sorry, darling, for everything," he said, his voice warm, caressing her senses. "I felt so awful when you left here. I wanted to beg you to come back."

"Why didn't you?" she asked.

"I don't know. I don't understand what's going on with me. When I met Summer she screamed, didn't want me near her. All I could think about was that you'd have done a much better job than I did. You would have known instinctively what to do."

Feeling closer to Lucas than she had since all of this

began, she held the phone tighter. "Lucas, why did you have an affair?"

She heard his sudden intake of breath and waited to see if he'd answer her.

"I want to tell you the truth, but are you sure you want to hear what I have to say?"

"Yes. I am." Her knees threatening to give out on her, she sat down on the sofa.

"Okay, but what I have to say is going to sound totally selfish." He cleared his throat. "I'm sure you weren't aware of this, but I seldom felt you were hearing me about anything other than trying to get pregnant."

"I always listened to you."

Lucas didn't say a word for a few minutes. "Do you have any idea how many times I tried to get you to go on vacation? And each time you'd insist that you couldn't go because you had to be near your gynecologist."

"I was afraid of being very far from my doctor. Why was a vacation so important?"

"Because I wanted you to focus your attention on me, on us and our marriage."

"I did. Having a baby was important to both of us."

"Yes. But many times, I felt as if you weren't even aware of me except as the man who could get you pregnant."

There was a long pause while she thought about what he'd said. "You really felt I ignored you except when we were trying to get pregnant," said.

"I did. I worked, came home and all we seemed to do was talk about getting pregnant. I felt as if what I wanted or needed really didn't matter."

"But Lucas, you had your work. You had your life outside this house. I had nothing...nothing but the hope that we would finally conceive."

"And that's why I kept my feelings to myself. Do you have

any idea how many times I simply wanted to hold you in my arms, to have you fall asleep in my arms, not from the effort of getting pregnant but because we loved each other and needed to hold each other close?"

Feeling the sincerity of his words across the connection, she began to see that maybe... "I was obsessed with getting pregnant. Is that what you're saying?"

He gave a huge sigh of relief. "Yes. After years of being together, the Carolyn I fell in love with seemed to have changed, and I didn't know how to deal with it. I was lonely, Carolyn. I needed you back with me."

"I was lonely too. You can only have so many lunches with friends, and shopping trip to the mall."

"I was *so* lonely," he whispered.

"And now you have a little girl."

"We have a little girl, Summer."

"A little girl who came out of an affair you had," she said.

A moment of quiet fell between them. "Lucas, I wish I could tell you that with time and effort, I might be able to forgive you. But I'm not sure if I'll ever be at that point, to feel it in my heart to forgive what you've done."

For a few moments, she feared that he might not answer, and it tore at her with a force she could never have imagined. What if she'd gone too far in what she'd said?

"Carolyn, I would like to be able to tell you that I will never hurt you again. But that's not possible. I've hurt you already. But I want you to believe that there isn't anything I wouldn't do to make this up to you. I haven't worked out exactly how to do that, but believe me, I'm going to try. I need you more than I could ever have imagined. Not just because of Summer, but because you're you. You make my life worthwhile."

A shudder ran through her at his words. "Oh, Lucas, if only none of this had happened," she whispered.

"But it did," he said, sadness tingeing his words.

CHAPTER NINE

Although some of the things they'd talked about last night were painful, Carolyn felt a little better this morning. The call had given her hope that they might be able to work things out between them.

Just as she finished tidying the bedroom and placing clothes in the laundry hamper, the phone rang. Lucas. She hadn't expected to hear from him so soon. "Did you get any rest?" she asked, falling into her old habit of being concerned for him.

"I did a little, not much. I miss you. I'm worried about how I'm going to cope with Summer."

"I miss you, too."

"I feel so lost, Carolyn. So confused and Summer...well she's...she's not what I expected. I mean. She gets upset whenever I go near her."

"It's going to take time, Lucas. She's been through a lot, the dear little girl..."

"I talked to Brad yesterday. I thought that maybe if I drove to Concord today, we could talk about all this, find a way to work things out."

"I'd like that so much, darling. To be honest, I spent part of the night thinking of ways to fix things, and so if you are willing to come here, I'd like to see you as soon as possible," he said, his voice radiating the old enthusiasm.

"How is Summer?" she asked.

"Lisa suggested that I might consider having Summer see a child psychologist. I hadn't thought of that. For now, I'd like to see if I could gain her trust, have her be willing to spend time with me...with us."

Carolyn heard the uncertainty in his words and remembered her promise to herself to keep in mind that Lucas had no family member to confide in or rely upon the way she did. "Lucas, you haven't been part of her daily life. She sees you as a stranger, and it will be a big change for her to see you as anything other than that. But I'm sure it will eventually work out."

"If you were here with me, I know we could work this out," he said.

She suddenly felt shy and uncertain. She'd never behaved this way around Lucas, this new thing of holding back. She'd always rushed in to support him in whatever he was doing.

"I can't wait for you to get here," he said. She heard the loneliness in his voice.

The familiarity of being needed by him drew her. "I'm ready to go now, so about two hours maybe."

He gave a protracted sigh. "I'll be waiting right here for you. Truthfully, I spent a miserable night without you."

"Me, too," she confessed.

"Carolyn, please drive carefully," he murmured in her ear.

"I will. I have to pack, then I can get on the road," she said.

"Can you bring me a couple of pairs of jeans and a couple of shirts? I didn't bring much in the way of clothes."

"Sure."

After she hung up, she realized she wanted Lucas to come

home with her. Their conversation made her feel they might find a compromise, if they were to sit down with a counselor to talk out their concerns about how Summer had come into their lives and how it had affected their marriage.

As she packed, her mind focused on what lay ahead, her thoughts filled uncertainty. What if she couldn't accept Summer into her life? What if she was a hurtful reminder of Lucas's infidelity? She felt guilty for feeling that way, but she couldn't help it.

One thing she knew for certain, she had to talk to him about all of this and what it meant for her. How could she get him to see her point of view? If they were to get through this with their marriage intact, they had to be totally honest about how they felt.

Hours later, she pulled into the driveway she'd left so hurriedly yesterday. Lucas met her at the door, his arms outstretched. "Oh, Carolyn. I've missed you so much."

She walked into his embrace feeling his warmth, breathing in his scent. He held her tight as he rocked her back and forth.

"I missed you, too, Lucas. Last night was the loneliest night of my life," she whispered into his cotton shirt, soaking in the newly scrubbed scent of his body. "Where did you stay last night?"

Still holding her tight, he led her into the house and along the hall to the kitchen. "I stayed here. Lisa thought it might help if I was around when Summer got up this morning. Lisa has gone shopping and Summer is at kindergarten. We've got the house to ourselves. Larry Knowles called to say he'd like to see me to start the process of working out the estate details. I want you to go with me," he said, drawing her into a kiss that made her knees weak with desire.

He pulled back and smiled into her eyes. "I've got coffee ready to go, and I went to the local bakery and got your favorite sandwich, Swiss cheese and ham with mayo and mustard."

"I'm famished. Did you get yourself a sandwich, as well?" she asked, slipping into her old behavior of thinking about him first. Yet it felt so easy, so natural. She shrugged off her concern that he might expect things to go back to the way they were. She had to believe that Lucas wouldn't let that happen.

He got two plates out of the cupboard and put them on the island. "I did. I ate earlier. The lawyer appointment isn't until two o'clock, so we have time."

Carolyn watched her husband, thinking about what she wanted to say. She knew how important Summer was to him, but she needed him to understand how she felt about it all. "Lucas, I think we need to be very clear on what we want to do."

He looked up from cutting her sandwich in half. "Of course, we need to be clear. But I'm not sure if you mean it the way I do."

"I mean Summer is a little girl who has never lived anywhere but in this house. We live miles away, with a life that we've made for the two of us, a life that never included a child, despite our wishes. At the very least, we will have to childproof the house. We'd have to find a pediatrician, a dentist who is good with children, a kindergarten, so many things will need to be decided."

"But once she's over the worst of it, Summer will be fine. Children adapt easily," Lucas said, as he studied her. "You don't see it that way, do you?"

"What I see is a child who will need a lot of care and attention in a loving, familiar environment. That environment isn't our home where nothing is familiar to her. It's here with her nanny."

"But what about us? We have been waiting most of our

marriage for a child. Now we have one," Lucas said, a bewildered look on his face.

"It's not just about having a child in our lives. It's about doing right for her and for us. That all takes planning and caring, Lucas. And so far we've done none of it."

"I don't understand," he said, his eyebrows drawn together as he poured the coffee and brought the cups and cream to the counter between them.

"This is a huge change for both of us. We'll have to make sacrifices to make sure that Summer is cared for and happy."

"But that's the whole point. We now have a child. We are a family," he said, leaning on the counter.

"Lucas, I don't know how to say this. I'm not sure I can accept Summer as my child. I...I... She belongs to you and Deidre."

Lucas stared across the glossy surface of the counter at her. "She belongs with you and me. Deidre's gone. She's not coming back. She left her child in our care. Deidre wasn't part of our lives, but we've been given the gift. Something good has come out of Deidre's death. At least, that's how I see it."

Carolyn took a deep breath, preparing herself to offer up what she felt. Crossing her fingers that Lucas would listen, she said, "That's not how I see it. I need time to accept her into our lives. She is a part of you, and I respect that. But she's not a part of me. I can't have a child, and I'm afraid that having Summer with us would be a constant reminder of your...."

Lucas blew out an impatient sigh. "Carolyn, how can I convince you that Deidre was never part of my life? The only really good thing that came out of that relationship was Summer."

"Lucas, please understand; we need time together to adjust to having a child in our lives. Would it be possible to leave Summer here with Lisa while you and I go home and talk this all out?"

"Are you saying you don't want Summer?" he asked, frustration tingeing his words.

"That's not what I said at all. What I said was I need to be sure that taking Summer into our lives is the right thing for us. We have so many problems we need to work on. This is all so sudden. I need to feel that we are doing the right thing for Summer and for us. I need us to talk it all out, rather than jump in so fast."

"The right thing? This isn't about right or wrong. This is about my daughter, our daughter. Carolyn, you're overreacting to all this. Don't let what happened years ago influence how you feel about Summer. This is our life. We have a child. What we both have wanted all along."

"But what you did back then is now influencing everything in our life, in my life. You had an affair, which you didn't tell me about. You find out you have a daughter from that affair and I'm supposed to jump onboard without a moment's thought or hesitation. I'm your wife. I was your wife before Deidre and before this child. I need you to support me in this, to give me time to adjust."

He pushed away from the counter, folded his arms over his chest. "I don't know what to say. You want me to leave Summer here while we go home and work on you adjusting to having a child in our lives when we've waited years for this opportunity. I don't get it," he said.

"I can't simply ignore what you and Deidre did to my life, to my faith in you. It's this simple. Either I'm part of this decision or I'm not," she said, sadness filling her heart.

"Carolyn, I can't abandon Summer. And that's what it would feel like if I went home with you now. But if you stay here with me, I'm willing to spend time working through this with you, reassuring you in any way I can."

"But how can we do that when we are caring for Summer, and all the she needs?" she asked, feeling miserable and alone.

"Are you afraid I'm taking Summer out of some sort of loyalty to Deidre?" he asked, his dark eyes intent on hers.

"Are you?"

"No. She's my child, our child."

"But how can that be when we haven't given ourselves time to get used to all this? I feel like you're expecting me to simply go along with what you want."

"That's not true. I want you to be part of this, but I can't abandon my daughter."

"I'm not asking you to abandon her."

"Then what are you saying?" he asked.

"I want you to listen to my side of things. I want us to work through this alone together. You said Summer isn't warming to you. Let's give her time and ourselves time," she said, her voice failing her as sobs shook her whole body. Through her tears, she searched for her purse. "This was a mistake coming here. A mistake."

"Don't say that, Carolyn," Lucas pleaded, going to her and holding her while she cried. He'd been so glad to see her when she drove in the driveway. Last night's conversation had been so open and caring, yet so laden with things that neither could say. He'd been thrilled to have her return to him, and he'd foolishly believed they could agree to have Summer return home with them.

Holding her close, he whispered, "I never meant to hurt you. I am as confused by all of this as you are. Not long ago I was running my business, we were having a little break in Boston."

"Because you wanted to break the news to me about the lawyer's letter."

"Yes. And then the phone call that changed everything."

She looked up at him, her cheeks pale and damp with tears. "Don't you see, Lucas? We've had so much to deal with in such a short time. We need to stop and think about all this, just the two of us. What difference will a week make in Summer's life? Isn't a delay while we talk this out better than our marriage suffering and Summer being caught in the middle?"

He held her shoulders as his eyes searched her tear-stained face. "Carolyn, I love you. I didn't realize that you felt this way. But you don't know how it felt last night to watch Summer, to feel that visceral connection to someone, someone who is totally dependent on me, what I do and how I do it. For the first time in my life, I'm confused, uncertain. And yet I've never felt this alive. Summer's a lovely little girl and I'm sure you will fall in love with her. Just wait until she gets home from kindergarten."

"I don't think that would be a good idea."

"Why not?"

"You still don't get it, do you?" She glanced at him and the sadness in her expression crushed his heart. "You want us to include a little girl in our lives while I'm still trying to cope with the relationship you had."

"It seems that every time I say something it comes out all wrong," he said, feeling lost, adrift and afraid that he was about to lose her.

"And I need to know that my feelings matter," she said.

"They do."

"Then listen to me. I need for us to take this slow, to talk this out together before we decide to take her home with us. This is a big decision for both of us. It will change our lives, our relationship, forever."

She couldn't be suggesting that he walk away from

Summer, leave her here on her own without family, could she? "But Carolyn I can't walk away from Summer."

"I'm simply suggesting that you come home with me. Summer will be fine with Lisa for a little bit and we work out a plan, look at our options. And if we decide to become parents, we find a kindergarten for Summer. We get our house ready for a little girl, not the infant we expected." She paused, then said slowly, "And we start proceedings to adopt her...if that's what we decide we want to do. In the meantime, she's safe and content here with Lisa."

"Carolyn, there is no decision to be made about whether or not we take Summer. The decision is when and how," he said, his heart surging in his chest as he began to see what was going on here. Carolyn was worried over things that were easily fixed. "You and I and Summer will be a family. Together we will arrange for everything Summer needs."

Carolyn's expression was despondent as she looked at him before turning away. "I am *not* Summer's mother. Her mother just died. If we're to be Summer's family, if that's the best resolution for all of us, you and I first have to agree on how we do it. If we're not, we'll only make your daughter unhappy. Is that what you want?"

Hurt, like a dull blade, jabbed at his heart. "I don't want anyone to be unhappy, especially not you," he said, feeling the situation slip out of his control.

"Then come home with me. Call Mr. Knowles and reschedule your meeting." She took his hand in hers, her skin warm and inviting. "We have so much to consider. If we are to get through all of this, we need to go to counseling."

"But why is counselling necessary if we love each other and want to be a family? Carolyn, don't do this to me. I already feel guilty that I had an affair and that I didn't know about Summer. I could have been here for her, but I wasn't. I can't make that right. But I... We've got a chance now to do what she needs."

"Your lack of involvement in Summer's life was Deidre's decision and out of your control."

He clutched her hand tighter. "That's true. And now I've got a chance to make it up to her by being with her. She's just a little girl. She's confused and missing her mom. I can help her. You can, too."

Carolyn pulled her hand away. "Lucas, it's clear that you and I can't resolve this standing here. Please come home with me and let's work this out between us."

"I love you with all my heart, Carolyn. But I can't leave Summer, not right now."

She turned her face to his, the look of longing in her eyes cutting straight to his heart. "Is that it? You're going to stay here with Summer rather than coming home with me?"

Aware that things were going terribly wrong, he fought to make her understand. "Carolyn, it's not that simple."

"It is. Either you love me enough to put my feelings first, or you don't."

"That's not fair!"

She stepped away from him. "But not enough. Not enough to make you change your mind. I came here to convince you that we needed to sort things out, for our sakes as well as for Summer's. It's pretty clear to me that I've wasted my time," she said, her voice catching.

"You haven't wasted your time. I do want to talk, but I can't leave Summer here by herself."

"She's not by herself. She's with the one person in her life she loves best. You said yourself she is shy around you, doesn't trust you. If you gave her a little time, it would be better for both of you. While she's adjusting to her life without her mother, you and I could be working out a plan that provides for Summer's needs."

"Providing for her needs? Are you suggesting we aren't what Summer needs?"

"I'm not suggesting anything, only that we sit down, just the two of us, and work this out between us," she said, her voice so soft he could barely hear her.

"Why did you come here if you weren't willing to help me bring Summer home?" he asked, barely hiding his annoyance. "Was all that talk about having a child just talk?"

She glared at him. "How dare you say that? You really don't want to change anything at all. I came here to talk this out and you're being totally selfish and unreasonable," she said, turning to go, her shoulders rigid.

When she got to the door, she turned to face him. "So, I guess that's it. There is nothing left to talk about. I'm going home, Lucas."

CHAPTER TEN

Hours later, with Carolyn's words still ringing in his ears, Lucas pulled into the parking lot at Larry Knowles's office. He hadn't known what to do or where to turn after Carolyn left. He felt hollow, cut off from everything he'd known and loved, adrift trying to make sense of it all. He'd been thankful for the meeting with the lawyer, anything to distract him from what had occurred between Carolyn and him.

Hearing the details of Deidre's will might help him better understand why she chose to do what she did, and maybe a hint as to why she'd not told him about Summer.

After he entered the building he was shown directly into the lawyer's office.

"So good to see you again," the lawyer said, coming around his desk to shake hands. "We'll get down to business. I've made a copy for you and will go through the major provisions set out in it."

Lucas picked up the document, reminded of how easily life can be summed up in a few pages of instructions for the beneficiary. "I wish I'd known Deidre better," he said, scanning the pages.

"How's that? You and she had a relationship, didn't you?"

"I don't know what she told you. My company did work with Deidre's. Our intimate relationship amounted to one weekend. A weekend that never should have happened." He looked across the desk at the lawyer. "I don't know why I'm telling you that, other than I feel guilty that I didn't know about Summer before Deidre passed away. I didn't know Deidre was pregnant. I never heard from her again after that weekend five years ago. I guess that's part of why I was so shocked when you called to tell me I was named as Summer's guardian."

Larry leaned back in his chair. "That's interesting. Deidre didn't go into the details of her connection to you, although your reaction to my initial phone call made me suspect you'd had very limited contact with her."

He rubbed his chin in thought. "Before I go through the various provisions, I'd like to tell you a couple things about Deidre that you may not have known. She always had to be in control, set the agenda. She was tough, hardworking and always very careful about whom she allowed close to her. As her friend, no one was more surprised than I was when she came to see me about her will. I'm probably overstepping my bounds, but I don't think she ever intended to have you find out about Summer. I think, like most people, she never believed she'd die young."

"Why would she do such a thing?" Lucas asked.

"Deidre wanted Summer to herself. I'm guessing here, but I believe it had to do with being an only child herself. She had told me she wanted a child, and when Deidre wanted something, she usually got it. I don't think she had many relationships. I was one of only a handful of friends. In my experience with Deidre, she was one of those people who made her decisions based on her needs at the time."

Lucas remembered that weekend, the way Deidre came on to him, seducing him with determination and eagerness. He'd been totally surprised by her attitude and her clear intention to have sex, even though he didn't have any condoms with him. He had never slept around on Carolyn, so had no need for such protection. Still, Deidre had assured him she was on birth control. Was it possible she'd misled him? If the lawyer was right, had Deidre intentionally gotten pregnant?

As he stared at the document, not reading a word of it, his mind scrambled over his memories of that weekend, the wild sex, the total freedom and excitement.

A sickening feeling flooded him, forcing him to face the ugliness of it all. Not only had he cheated on his wife, destroying the trust between them and breaking his vow to the only woman he'd ever loved, but he'd done it without thinking of the other possible repercussions of having sex.

Because of his actions, a little girl had been born without the advantage of having a father in her life. And now, because of Deidre's decision to name him as guardian for her daughter, his marriage might not survive and Summer might still end up without a mother. What a hell of a mess!

He sighed inwardly as he met Larry's inquiring gaze. "Obviously Deidre liked being in charge, so what else has she dictated?"

The lawyer eyed him. "What does your wife think of all this? It must be very difficult for her."

"She didn't know about the affair. And now she doesn't believe I didn't have any contact with Deidre since it happened. I can't blame her given the circumstances. Quite frankly, my marriage is in trouble."

Larry Knowles shook his head slowly. "I'm sorry for you

and your wife, but my concern is for Summer. She deserves a stable environment. She has Lisa, of course, but no family to speak of." The lawyer stared straight at him. "If you agree to the terms of the will, you have a huge responsibility."

"And if I don't take Summer, my daughter will become a ward of the state and put up for adoption," he said, returning the lawyer's demanding gaze.

"She will."

"I messed up and hurt two people who were completely innocent. Now I have to make things right for them. I love both of them very much. I never knew what it felt like to be a father, and now I have a child who needs me. I plan to take good care of her and to prove to my wife how much I love her."

The lawyer's expression softened. "Then let's get to the will. Deidre left an estate of a little over five million, most of which is invested with a professional investment group here in the city. I have all that information when you're ready to deal with it. I have all the documents ready for you to sign as the guardian. Deidre wanted you to move into her house."

"But Deidre knew I had a wife, that I lived outside of Boston. Why would she think I'd move here?"

"Again, Deidre looked at things from her perspective and what she wanted for Summer. Knowing her as I did, she probably thought that the combination of money and her home would entice you to move here. But I'm only guessing." He shifted in his chair. "Why don't I go through the will? If you have questions, we can address them. Would that work?"

An hour later, after he'd signed all the paperwork at the brokerage firm, and set up new bank accounts, he headed back to Deidre's house, relieved that all of that was finished. There would be further decisions to make later, but the urgent details and paperwork had been settled.

Watching Summer this morning before she left the house

had made him even more determined to be a good father. With her bright red curls and blue eyes, her instant smile and the adorable way she talked and played with Lisa, he couldn't take his eyes off her.

It was true that, so far, she'd avoided any direct contact with him, but he believed with all his heart that, given time, he could change that, He looked forward to the day he could hold her and play with her the way Lisa did. Until then, he would take it slow, be there for her and make certain that her life was as close to normal as possible. That meant staying here for at least a few days to get everything organized.

He heard the back door open and moved off the kitchen stool he'd been sitting on. Summer came in, tugging on Lisa's hand, a ready smile on her face. When she saw him, she slowed, stopped and stared at him. Without saying a word, he smiled at her. She gave him a tiny smile back, and his heart soared. He was making progress.

Lisa put the backpack on the counter, then went to the fridge. "What would you like for a snack?" she asked Summer. "What about pita and hummus?"

Lucas had never eaten hummus in his life, but he was certainly willing to try. If eating hummus would give him a starting point with his daughter, he'd eat a gallon of it.

He waited to see what Summer would do.

She rushed across the room to the fridge and took the food from Lisa's hands. "I'm hungry," she said, placing the food on the counter and climbing up on a stool next to him.

"Let me help you with that," he said, reaching toward her.

She looked anxiously at him out of the corner of her eye, her lower lip jutting out. Was she going to cry? He hoped not. He'd seen enough tears for one day. "Can I have some of that?" he asked.

Summer blinked. A slight smile slowly turned up the corners of her mouth. "Mommy says we should all eat healthy," she said, popping her thumb into her mouth as her eyes moved to Lisa, who was putting the food on a plate.

"Your mom is right. We should all eat healthy," he said.

"Can I have juice, please?" she asked.

"Certainly," Lisa answered, going to the cupboard and returning with what seemed to Lucas to be a lot of similar small boxes with colorful cartoon characters on them.

Summer reached for the plate and slid it across to him. "We can share."

His heart beat hard in his chest at the kind gesture. "Thank you. I'd really like that."

They settled in to enjoy the snack while Lisa started to prepare dinner. Watching Summer eat and chat with Lisa, Lucas spent the most enjoyable time he'd had since coming here. He had to believe that everything would work out. He'd make sure it did. And the hummus wasn't half-bad, either.

He was laughing at Summer's antics with a piece of pita when Lisa spoke. "Lucas, we need to talk."

"Sure. Now?"

"Summer, sweetie, how would you like to finish your snack while you watch SpongeBob SquarePants?" Lisa asked as she gathered the remainder of the food and took it to the family room. Summer gave him a quick smile as she slid off the stool. "Do you like SpongeBob?" she asked him.

"Ah... I don't think I've ever seen it," he said, realizing that he was going to have to learn all about Summer's likes and dislikes, and clearly her favorite TV programs.

She stared at him. "Everyone watches SpongeBob Square Pants. It's funny." She giggled as she followed Lisa into the family room.

When Lisa returned, she had a concerned look on her face. "I had a call from my family while I was waiting for Summer. My mother has been taken to the hospital, and I have to go."

"I'm sorry to hear that. What can I do?"

She looked at him a little strangely. "Nothing. You'll have your hands full with Summer. Having lost her mother and without me here, Summer will need all the love and support you can give her."

He had to care for Summer? On his own? The knowledge slammed into him with the force of a sledgehammer.

"I'm afraid I'll screw up. I mean, I'm just learning this whole parenting thing. Summer is still very uncomfortable around me. It's not a good idea to leave her alone with just me, is it?" he asked, his heart pounding hard against his ribs.

Lisa gave him a quick glance. "There really isn't anyone else I can call on, and I have to go. If you need help, I'm sure Deidre's friend Valerie Henson could step in, but she works full-time and has kids of her own," she said as she continued to peel carrots at the sink."I'm afraid it's up to you."

"I..." What was he going to do?

"Your wife is here. She could help you."

"No. Carolyn went back home. She's having difficulty coping with all the change going on in our life."

Lisa turned to him, a concerned look on her face. "I'm sorry to hear that, but I have no choice. I have to go. I'll leave you with a detailed list of instructions. And any contacts you might need are posted on the fridge." She pointed to what looked like sheets and sheets of information. "I'm sure you'll be fine."

She finished preparing dinner before going to pack her suitcase. Still trying to process Lisa's news, Lucas watched in horror as Lisa knelt next to Summer in the family room. "I have to go away for a couple days to see my family, but I'll be back as soon as possible."

"Don't go!" Summer sobbed, throwing herself into Lisa's arms. Lisa picked her up and carried her to the kitchen where Lucas stood transfixed by the enormity of this situation. He hadn't imagined that he might have to care for Summer alone. He'd been counting on Lisa and Carolyn to be around and do the things little girls needed done.

How was he to manage the care of a child he knew so little about? He had no experience with children. He had no siblings, no cousins his age and had never been around young kids.

Summer clung to Lisa. The longer her misery continued, the more Lucas wished fervently that Lisa might change her mind or at least take Summer with her. "Are you sure this is a good idea, I mean, leaving me with me?"

"We don't have a choice," Lisa said, her voice low to prevent Summer from hearing what she said. She glanced at her watch. "And I have to get going." She gave him a worried look.

"I'll figure it out," he conceded as he moved closer to Summer, smiling as if his life depended on it.

For what seemed like a lifetime, Summer eyed him from under her teary eyelashes. Eventually, she pulled her thumb from her mouth, hiccoughing and sniffling before putting her arms out to him. Tentatively, he reached for her, still waiting for her to changer her mind and bury her face in Lisa's chest. When she didn't, he took her in his arms, patting her narrow shoulders.

What should he do now? He'd heard from someone say, a long time ago, that it was soothing to a child to carry them around the house looking at whatever caught the child's attention. He began moving from room to room. "Look outside," he said, pointing at the American flag fluttering on the flagpole near the garage. "What's that?"

"Flag," she said before popping her thumb back into her mouth, resting her tiny head on his shoulder and snuggling close. Love for his daughter, like a living thing, filled his chest, expanding to fill his body, shaking him to his core.

He was walking around the kitchen, pointing things out for Summer to name when Lisa appeared with her purse and a small suitcase: And it struck him. He really *was* going to be one hundred percent responsible for this little girl. "You're leaving now," he said, hearing the raw anxiety in his voice.

"I am." Lisa looked at Summer, who promptly pulled away from Lucas and reached for Lisa.

"I go with you," Summer said as Lisa wrapped her arms around his little girl.

"You have to stay here with your dad. I'll be back as soon as I can, and in the meantime, you be good, okay?" Lisa said, kissing her cheek.

Summer pulled her thumb from her mouth. "No! You stay!" she demanded, tears spilling down her cheeks.

"I have to go, honey," Lisa murmured, her eyes filling with tears as she held the little girl. She looked over at Lucas. "Can you take her for me?"

Tentatively, he reached for Summer, who immediately began to cry harder. Lucas waited, not knowing what to do, fearing that Summer would not stop crying when Lisa left the house.

"I have to go, Summer," Lisa said again, and this time she passed Summer to him. The child struggled in his arms and managed to slide to the floor, following Lisa to the door. Lucas went after her, trying to remain calm while he figured out his next move.

"Please stay here with me," he said to Summer as he managed to pick her up again, evoking loud wails.

Lisa turned, a desperate look on her face. "Find one of her favorite teddy bears," she said as she turned quickly, opened the door and walked out, to another yelp of protest from Summer.

"I don't know which bears are her favorite," he said to the closed door.

Summer scrambled out of his arms, fleeing to the window in the living room that looked out on the driveway. "Weeza!" she screamed, climbing over the back of the sofa.

He went to her, unsure if he should try to pick her up and comfort her. Hoping to calm his little girl, he glanced around the room looking for a toy that might soothe her. In a corner, he spotted the black teddy bear perched precariously on the edge of a tapestry-covered bench. He grabbed the furry toy and offered it to Summer.

At first, she ignored him, sucking her thumb and hiccoughing. When she did glance his way, she stared at him suspiciously. He waited, his throat constricted with worry at the possibility that Summer might simply continue to cry, and he wouldn't be able to comfort her.

Seconds later her tiny hand grabbed the bear before turning away from him and nestling into the sofa while she patted the bear's back.

What should he do now? He glanced around, trying to figure out if he could get her back to the TV in the family room. Not ideal parenting, but the TV might distract her and give him time to work something out.

"Summer, would you let me watch SpongeBob Square-Pants with you?" he asked, mentally crossing his fingers that the program was still on.

She peered up at him, sighed and offered her bear to him. "Blackie and I will show you."

He took the bear, grateful for the change in his daughter, and followed her to the TV. Cartoon characters he'd never seen before who seemed to live under the water flashed on the screen. How weird was that? He edged down beside her on the sofa. "So, tell me about this show. Who is SpongeBob?"

Relief whirled around him as he listened to her animated description of what seemed to be a bunch of characters making Krabby Patties while hurling insults at each other and throwing things. But he really didn't care about the storyline as long as Summer seemed content and was not crying. For now, he was happy to sit with her, watch her as she pointed and laughed at the antics of the characters.

Carefully he eased back on the sofa, hoping that Summer might snuggle next to him for a few minutes. Before long, she glanced at him, her gaze shifting to his lap. He took that to mean she wanted him to hold her. When he opened his arms, she climbed onto his lap, and not too long after, she fell asleep on his shoulder.

What should he do now? Would she sleep until her bedtime, then stay awake half the night crying for Lisa, or worse, her mother? He didn't have any idea and it frightened him. All he could be sure of was that, for now, things were quiet.

A little later, she awoke suddenly, rubbed her eyes. "I'm hungry," she said, sitting up straight and staring at him.

"What would you like to eat?" he asked.

"Tomato soup and crackers," she said, sliding off his lap and heading to the kitchen, dragging Blackie the bear behind her.

"Can I have some, too?" he asked, following her to the kitchen.

She raised her arms up to him. "Yes. But only four crackers," she said, holding up four fingers as he lifted her into his arms.

"Do you help Lisa make dinner?"

"Yes. I sit there." She pointed to the stool closest to the kitchen sink.

"Want to sit there now?" he asked.

"Yes."

He was pleased to make her dinner and watch as she slurped the soup. He didn't realize that little kids liked soup, but his daughter certainly did. Upstairs, he ran a bath and helped Summer into it. He sat on the floor beside the tub and watched as she splashed and played with plastic fish and other assorted creatures.

Wanting to get her to bed so he could relax for a while, he held out a towel to Summer. "I think it's time to get out of the tub, don't you?"

For a minute, her lips formed a pout and he held his breath.

Please don't cry. Please.

"Yes!" Summer's face lit up with a smile. He scooped her up and started down the hall to her bedroom.

"We'll get you into your pajamas, and then I'll read you a story," he said.

She pointed to her mother's room as they reached the door. Oh. No. "You want to go in there?" he asked, preparing himself for the onslaught of tears he was certain would erupt if they went into Deidre's room. "Are you sure you don't want to get your pajamas on now? We could look in your mother's room later."

Summer gave her head a vigorous shake sending damp curls cascading over her face.

"Okay." He carried her into the room, the evening sky spreading shades of pink and

gold across the cream-colored duvet. Summer pointed to the mantel over the fireplace.

"Mommy's photo. You want to look at that," he said, dreading what would happen next.

Summer reached toward the mantel, picking up the photo of him next to the one of Deidre. "Daddy," she said, hugging it close, her thumb making its way into her mouth, but not before she smiled into his face.

His heart slowed to a steady thump as he held her tight in his arms. His life seemed to stand still as he met his daughter's gaze. An emotion he couldn't name swamped him, and he knew only that he'd never felt it before. "Yes. Daddy," he said, as tears of joy ran unfettered down his face.

"Don't cry," she said, her expression anxious.

"I'm crying because I'm happy," he whispered taking the photo from her tiny hands and gingerly putting it on the mantel.

"No!" Summer reached for the photo, taking it in her pudgy hands. "Mine!"

"You want to keep that?" he asked, marveling at how easy she was to hold.

"My room," she said, leaning back in his arms and peeking up at him from under her dark lashes.

In her room, she put on her pajamas and climbed into bed, still clutching his photo in her hands. Watching her, he knew he would remember every detail of this moment for the rest of his life.

Abruptly, his thoughts turned to Carolyn. He wanted to share this moment with her. She, better than anyone he knew, would appreciate how he was feeling. But first, he had to be sure that Summer was settled. "Do you want me to read to you?" he asked, following Lisa's instructions about the bedtime routine.

"No. Mommy reads to me," she said, her eyes dark pools of worry. "I want Mommy."

Lucas felt so sorry for his little girl, and so helpless. Nothing would change the sad truth that her mother would never be with her again, would never hold her or read to her.

He knelt beside the bed. "Well, maybe you could show me your favorite book, and maybe I could read to you sometime. Maybe even tomorrow night?" he asked, fearing that she would simply continue to cry. If she did, what would he do? There was no one to turn to. He could call Carolyn, but what could she do over the phone?

Slowly a small smile started on Summer's face, pushing

her cheeks up into tiny pink globes. Was she going to be okay? "Can I take the photo?" he asked, hoping to smooth the tiny frown between her perfectly blue eyes.

Summer snuggled under the pink duvet, handing him the photo. "I'll put it on the bookcase?" he asked, unbelievably relieved that she seemed to be settling for the night.

She nodded, her thumb slipping into her mouth. He kissed her forehead, reveling in the softness of her skin and the fresh-scrubbed scent of her. Unfamiliar feelings he could not explain filled him. He'd never felt this way in his life. She gave him a sleepy smile as she snuggled beneath the sheets. He would do anything, make any sacrifice, for the little girl lying there looking up at him. Anything.

"See you in the morning," he whispered.

"Leave the door open," she murmured, her voice filled with sleep.

"Sure. I'll check on you a little later. Sweet dreams, princess."

He tiptoed out of the room, but not before he saw her eyelids slide closed. He took a deep breath, the first since he'd gotten her out of the tub. Overall, the evening had gone pretty well. Or, at least, he thought so. He'd be sure to check on her several times during the night, just in case. If she were afraid and lonely, would she get up and come into his room? Or would she go to her mother's room?

Back in his room, he reread the list of instructions that Lisa had left for him all sorts of information about Summer's daily life, things he hadn't imagined he'd need to learn so soon.

He called Carolyn, eager to tell her what had happened and talk about everything he was feeling. The past couple of hours had been a roller coaster, from his early fear that he couldn't cope to his conviction that he could do this. He could.

"Hi, Lucas," Carolyn said, her voice sounding strained.

"Are you okay?" he asked.

"I'm fine. What about you?"

"I'm doing okay, mostly. I wanted to tell you about Lisa and what's been going on," he said as he started to list off the events since she'd left earlier in the day.

Carolyn listened to Lucas talk about his daughter in excited, upbeat tones. Even the news that the nanny had to be off for a few days didn't seem to faze him. She was frankly amazed that Lucas hadn't called her the minute he knew Lisa had to leave.

"And you managed to get her into the tub?" she asked.

"She got in on her own. She knew which bubble bath her mom used. She got her own towel out of the linen closet, and she chose her own snack, which, by the way, she ate in the tub," he said, chuckling. "I had no idea what Ritz crackers looked like floating around in bubbles. And she is so sweet and funny. I just sat by the tub and watched her. Carolyn, you can't imagine what it felt like to have my daughter with me, to see her play in the bathwater and so many other things. I... Carolyn, I love her so much," he said, his voice low and filled with wonder.

"You're amazing. How did you do this on your own?"

"I nearly called you to help me, but I didn't dare leave Summer."

"I would have helped you if I could," she said, a part of her wishing that things were different between them. A part of her admiring his new-found ability to care for a child.

Could she have done what he did? She wasn't sure. She'd done a little babysitting and read books on child-rearing...many books on child-rearing. But would it have been easier for her?

"If only you'd stayed and met her," he said.

His words filled her with remorse and. She wished she'd been there with him, to see his little girl, but she would not have found it easy to witness his love for a child she felt so ambiguous about.

"I'm really pleased for you, Lucas," she said, struggling to sound upbeat, but all she could think about was that another woman had made her husband happier than she'd ever known him to be. Another woman had given him the child he wanted. "You sound very happy," she said.

He hadn't said a word about them or their relationship or the way things had been left between them a few short hours ago. Once she was home, she'd prayed that he would call, that they would talk a little. As evening approached, she'd grown anxious. They'd never let the sun go down on their anger. They'd always made up before going to sleep.

How could he not have wanted to talk to her before this? How many husbands have their wives walk out after an argument and not ask how they are doing?

"Carolyn, are you still there?" he asked.

"I am. I'm just a little sad and a little jealous, I suppose..."

"I'm sad that you weren't here with me to share these past few hours."

"I want to get to know Summer, too. I'm sure if we talk this all out sensibly, we can find a solution that works for all of us."

"I want that, as well. I was really down earlier today. After you left and I was finished with the lawyer, I realized that I was as much to blame, if not more so than Deidre for what happened. I should never have had sex with her. It was stupid and irresponsible. But I can't regret Summer. I don't know why Deidre didn't tell me about her, let me be involved, but that's over. I want us to move on, the three of us. Did I tell you that Summer held my photo and called me Dad?"

"She did?" Carolyn said, her throat twisting into a hard knot. Lucas had had the moment she'd dreamed of all her life that moment when her child called her Mom. "That's lovely for you."

"I... Whatever we decide, I don't want to ever be separated from Summer again."

"Not even for a few days while we sort things out between us?" she asked, feeling a sense of foreboding.

"I can't leave her. Lisa's been called a way. Her mother's very ill."

"Oh! I'm sorry to hear that. What are you going to do?"

There was a long pause before Lucas spoke. "Stay here. I have to, now. I didn't understand earlier why you wanted us to take it slow, think things through. I do now. But with Lisa gone for who knows how long, I have to look after Summer."

"I understand."

"And I would really like you here with me," he said, his voice tentative.

"I would like that. I feel...lonely."

"You're not alone. I'm here."

"And I hear what you're saying. You have to stay."

"Carolyn, a few weeks ago 'taking it slow' would have been my words. I'm the one who likes to sit back and deliberate on what to do and how to do it. But Carolyn, there's no problem here that I can see. What I'd like is to have you and Summer together. Believe me, all your worries will disappear. Would you consider that?"

"I'm not sure..."

"Carolyn, you were right. Summer needs to be here in her own home. She needs to stay in familiar surroundings. With Lisa gone, I'm all she has left."

"It must have been a little scary when Lisa left."

"I was terrified. I didn't know what I would do if Summer didn't stop crying. And she seemed almost afraid of me. It really hurt to see her that way. Carolyn, please come and be with us."

"Oh Lucas, I would love to be there but I can't make another trip only to have you behave the way you did the last time. I really need more time."

"So, that's it then? You won't come here to be with me?"

"I wish I could."

CHAPTER ELEVEN

After the phone call, Lucas had thrown himself into Summer's life while he waited for Lisa to return. He'd managed to get Summer off to kindergarten without a huge flood of tears, and he was navigating the whole which-book-to-read-at-night thing. It had seemed complicated in the beginning, but really came down to allowing Summer to deliberate in front of her bookshelves about which book he could read to her.

A neighbor had dropped by offering to help him if needed, and the postman had dropped off a parcel. Not knowing what to do with parcels addressed to Deidre, he opened the package to find half a dozen new outfits for Summer from an online store specializing in clothing for young girls. It was clear from the invoice that Deidre had spent an exorbitant amount of money. He looked them over, realizing that he had no idea what size Summer wore or where to buy clothes for her. For future reference, he made a note of the company and its address.

There had been moments in the past two days when he'd

wanted to call Carolyn. He wanted to, but he couldn't get past the fact that she'd refused to help him. She only seemed to be able to see all this from her perspective and what she wanted, and he didn't have the ability to cope with all of her concerns when his days were filled with learning to manage his daughter's life.

Besides, he had to believe that Carolyn would come around. She loved children and they now had a daughter. Once she could accept that and look forward to what their life now was, everything would work out. And if Carolyn could meet Summer, he knew she'd want to be part of her life.

Ultimately, what he needed to do was convince Lisa to move home with him, and that way Carolyn would see how wonderful everything could be. He didn't want to simply bring Summer into their lives and expect Carolyn to take over. It would be nice if he could, but that couldn't happen as long as Carolyn felt the way she did. Until she changed, Lisa would be a good buffer. And she would give Summer some continuity while she got used to living with them.

And his time here in Concord was causing problems at work. Brad had called with questions and decisions they needed to make, and he'd spent hours on the phone last evening after he put Summer to bed while they worked on the more urgent problems. It wasn't right for him to be away from work too long, especially when their marketing efforts to grow the business were paying off in substantial sales increases.

He checked his watch again. Lisa had called and said she'd be here by noon. He couldn't imagine what she'd say to his idea of moving with him and Summer, but he had to give it a try.

When Lisa walked through the door, she didn't waste any time. "Where's Summer?"

"She's at kindergarten," he said, surprised at the question.

"Seriously? I thought she'd want to stay home when she realized I wouldn't be here to take her. I always take her to school." Lisa looked around. "How did you make out otherwise? Did she cry a lot?"

"A little the first evening after you left. She really missed you."

Lisa's smile brightened. "I missed her, too. She's like my own daughter, and now with her mom gone..."

"How's your mom doing?"

"She had to have a stent put in, but she's doing okay."

"I'm glad to hear that." Lisa's presence would allow him to focus more on work, on the moving plan...and on Carolyn. "I wanted to talk to you about Summer and her future, if you have time."

Lisa perched on a stool in front of the kitchen island. "I have all the time in the world, or until Summer needs to be picked up."

"I'm thinking about taking Summer home with me. I've been working with the lawyer and a lot of Deidre's will has been settled. I really need to get back to my wife and my business. Of course, I want to take Summer with me."

Tears glistened in Lisa's eyes. "What about this house? What about Summer and her kindergarten?"

"I won't put the house on the market just yet. First, I want to have Summer's life in order, get her settled in my home. If she's really upset by the change, it might mean that we come back here, so I'll keep the house for now."

He glanced at her for approval, but saw none. "The thing is, I'd like you to come along. Summer would be happier with you in her life, and it would give you a chance to see where she will be living. I know it's important for you to see that Summer is settled in a good home. And it would make it easier for Carolyn and I to work things out. Not to mention my company business is suffering because I'm so far away. Would you consider coming with us?"

Lisa squared her shoulders. "When you put it that way, of course I'll come with you. It's important that some part of Summer's life remain constant. But you have to know that I have had other job offers, and if your wife will be staying home with Summer, you won't need me very long. I would like to be free to take another nanny position as soon as Summer is settled with you and your wife."

"I understand, and I appreciate you being frank with me."

"When do you plan to move?"

"Sometime in the next week. I haven't had a chance to look for a kindergarten near our home, but I'm sure Carolyn and I can find one."

"I don't mean to interfere, but your wife and I didn't hit it off when she was here. If my going with you should cause a problem, I won't stay more than a couple days. As much as I love Summer, she is not my child. She's yours. You have the final decision on everything related to her. And, to be honest, I don't want to live in a hostile environment."

He was once again surprised by Lisa's matter-of-fact tone. She obviously loved Summer, but the move would not be easy for her. "Summer is my first priority. But this has been very difficult for my wife, as she didn't know about my relationship with Deidre."

Lisa's eyebrows shot up. "What? You mean she only found out when Deidre died?"

He didn't want to tell this woman more than was necessary, but he did want to clear up any misconceptions. "Yes. I hadn't said anything because it was a long time ago, and that was the only time I broke my marriage vows. Finding out what I'd done was very hard on my wife."

"I had no idea..." Lisa said, a stern look on her face.

"We are working out our problems."

She gave him an odd look but said nothing. "I'll drive in my own car," she said. "That might be better for everyone."

"I'll call Carolyn."

Carolyn had just returned from the grocery store. She'd struggled to find something she wanted to eat, as her appetite had abandoned her after that last conversation with Lucas. She didn't know what to do about him, or about their marriage, in the light of his obsession with Summer.

She'd tried to talk to her brother about it, but Brad had had several work emergencies and had gone out of town on business. She wondered if Brad had spoken with Lucas about the backlog of work that wasn't getting done. If he had, she doubted that Lucas was listening. He was probably too preoccupied with his daughter to even notice the stress Brad was under.

Lucas certainly hadn't noticed anything about her during his last call. All he'd talked about was himself and his daughter.

She had just placed the last of the vegetables in the fridge when the phone rang.

Lucas. Taking a deep breath, she picked up. "Lucas, I am sorry I couldn't agree to go to Concord."

"That's okay. I understand how I must have made you feel. But I might I have the answer. I can't be away from you any longer, and I am so anxious for you to get to know Summer. I've decided to come home and bring Summer with me."

"You what?" she yelled in disbelief. "How can you take that child away from everything and everyone she knows so soon after her mother's death, with no plan on how to look after her? Lucas, you're not thinking straight. This isn't fair to Summer or to me or anyone else in your life. Brad needs you at work. You can't move Summer here when we're in this mess. I wouldn't be fair to anyone, but especially to her."

"Carolyn, I talked to Lisa and she's willing to move in with us and help with Summer, getting her settled and into a routine. Summer will be just fine with Lisa along.

"And how long can Lisa stay with us?" she asked.

To think he could bring a child into their home without discussing the arrangements with her was so hurtful she could hardly breathe. What had happened to Lucas? Why was he so determined to bring this child into their lives?

"She hopes to stay about a month. If that's all right?"

"Why didn't you talk this over with me first?"

"I thought you'd understand. Like you said, I need to get back to work, and I don't want to leave Summer. Lisa says she can help out for a while. We'll have to work out the details. I don't plan to be there for a week or so…"

"Is this how it's going to be, Lucas? You make one decision then another and I'm supposed to just fall in line." Her hands trembled so much she could hardly hold the phone.

"Carolyn, honey, please don't be upset. We can talk over the details, and when I get there you and I will sit down together and talk about all of this."

Tears began their steady movement over her cheeks, down into the corners of her mouth, tasting salty on her lips. "We'll talk, will we? Like the last time?"

"No. We will really talk. I promise."

Her heart beat slowly with the pain of knowing that he would be willing to talk to her now, when he was on his way back here with his daughter, putting her in the unbearable position of having his child in her home. "Lucas, this isn't what I wanted; you and me trying to talk while we work to adjust our lives to Summer and the issues that moving her would create. As far as I'm concerned you can do whatever you like. I won't be here."

His abrupt intake of breath reached across the connection. "You don't mean that. You wouldn't leave me. I love you with my whole heart. Look, whatever it takes, I'll do it."

"I've heard you say those words since the first phone call about Summer. But they're only words."

CHAPTER TWELVE

The sound of the dead connection stabbed Lucas like a knife. This couldn't be happening. What was he going to do without Carolyn? Glancing around at the messy counter and the load of laundry sitting by the door of the laundry room, he felt adrift and lost. He'd never faced anything like this.

Why had he rushed this? He could have stayed here for a while and given Carolyn time to adjust. Maybe he could have even gone home for a few days, talked to Carolyn and gotten caught up at work.

He should have given her time to adjust to what was happening. Why didn't he? Why didn't he talk to her about what they should do? He was beginning to wonder if he was losing it.

But in his heart, he wanted his little girl in his life so badly that he couldn't think of anything but her and what he wanted to do for her. Everything else paled in the face of those feelings.

"Is something going on?" Lisa asked, coming into the kitchen with another load of laundry.

He eyed the load. "Sorry I didn't get all the laundry done."

"Do you know how to do laundry?" she asked skeptically.

"Yes..." He didn't have a clue. Other than the years in college, his mother and then Carolyn had always done the laundry. "No. You're right. I haven't done laundry in a very long time."

"I suspect you haven't had to do much around the house," she said, eyeing the counter.

"Yeah. My wife stayed home. We wanted a family and I wanted her to be free to care for our children, not having to divide her time between work and family."

"Better for you, as well," she said. "Lucas, are you sure your wife wants me there with you and Summer?"

What was he going to tell her? He couldn't admit to himself that Carolyn had left him, let alone explain it to someone he hardly knew. But he had no choice if he wanted to leave for home tomorrow. "It's been a big adjustment for Carolyn. All of this."

"I should say. You didn't tell her about the affair. Did you talk to her about what you should do about Summer?"

"I tried to, but I didn't get it right."

"So she was okay with you coming home with Summer and me?"

"No. To be honest, she wasn't."

"Then why would you decide to do it without getting her support for the move?"

"I thought she'd go along with it." He scrubbed his face as realization dawned. "I've always assumed that Carolyn would go along because she always has. Even now... What am I going to do?"

Lisa placed her hands firmly on the island that separated them. "I don't know if it's such a good idea to take Summer to your home until you settle your differences with your wife. I can stay here with her, and keep her life as quiet and normal as possible while you and your wife figure out what you're going to do."

His stomach burned at the thought of leaving Summer. "Summer needs to be with me, and I have to get back to my work. We're really busy and I have to be there. I can't leave Summer, and she needs you to be with her as well. But I need to get home. I can't lose Carolyn." He willed her to understand.

She stared at him, her eyes dark. "You have gotten yourself into a terrible mess, haven't you?"

"I have. And it's my fault...all my fault."

"It is." Lisa squinted as if in thought. "I will go with you on the condition that you talk to your wife and work this out. I will not stay if you don't make a real effort to settle things with her."

His shoulders slumped in resignation. "I thought I had. That's how badly I've messed up. I thought she wanted what I wanted."

"It's my guess that, in your eagerness to take over Summer's life, you haven't been listening to Carolyn. If you'd been listening, you would not have allowed her to leave here without talking everything through. Why do you think I disappeared that first day? I could tell you two weren't on the same page over any of this. And anybody with half a brain would have seen how upset your wife was. If you ask me, you need to start over with her." She gave him a wry smile. "There. I'm done. But it had to be said. And one more piece of advice. Don't move Summer for a few more days. It's been only a few weeks since her mother passed away. Give her a little more time."

Lisa's words hit him hard. He was so self-centered. And he'd taken Carolyn for granted. "I don't want to do anything to upset Summer, but the truth is I need to get back to work. My business is suffering with me being away from the office."

"You can use Deidre's home office. It's completely equipped, including two desktop computers. You already have access to the Wi-Fi."

"I hadn't thought of that, but you're right, I could."

She walked ahead of him to Deidre's office, across the hall from the living room. The office looked much as it had five years ago, although the equipment had clearly been updated. With a stable network connection, he'd be able to access the company system. He wouldn't be able to do all of his work, but he'd make some inroads.

He could call Carolyn and arrange a Skype call with her. That way he could try again with her. It wasn't ideal, but it was the only thing he could think of at the moment. The only thing he knew for certain was that he couldn't make another mistake where Carolyn was concerned.

Carolyn was so relieved when Brad pulled into the parking lot of his condo. She had called him in tears after the conversation with Lucas. When her brother heard how upset she was, he'd told her to meet him there. He was at a meeting in Greenville, but he'd said he would be home as soon as possible.

She jumped out of her car and raced over to him.

"I'm sorry you're so upset. What's Lucas up to now?" he asked, pulling her close.

"I'm so happy to see you."

"I'll always be here for you, Sis," he said, hugging her tight. "It's kind of nice to have my baby sister need me."

"I'll always need you, silly," she murmured into his shirt.

"Not in recent times. Even with all your baby-making efforts, you kept your biggest worries to yourself," he said, clicking the locks on his truck key fob before starting up the walkway toward the condo entrance. "Let's go in so we can talk."

Once inside, he led her over to the sofa. "Now, spill the beans. You and Lucas are fighting about how he's behaving over Summer and Deidre, right?"

"Yes. It's as if he's taken complete control of our lives."

"Have you told him how you feel?"

"Yes,"

"What did he say?"

"That he was willing to talk, but that was after he'd left me feeling as if I didn't matter in his life."

Brad looked at her, his affection for her clear in his expression. "I'm here to encourage you to not let go of what you and Lucas have. I realize that's not easy, given what a mess he's managed to make of things, but you can't give up."

"What am I supposed to do? Every time we speak, it's all about his daughter, his concerns. I feel so angry at him'"

"That you clam up, right? You get angry and you walk away."

"That's not true!"

"Let me ask you something, and be honest with yourself."

"Go ahead," she said, feeling very uncomfortable with the conversation.

"Do you think there will ever come a day when you can forgive Lucas for what he did?"

"I don't know. There's so much between us that is good, but the past few weeks have left me unable to trust him. I don't believe in him anymore. I'd really like to have our old life back, but I realize that's not possible under the circumstances. We will always have a child he had with another woman in our lives. I'm not sure I can get past that."

"Oh, Sis, I wish I could kick Lucas's ass to Mars and back for what he did. Believe me, Lucas seriously regrets what he did. Hell. He's called me every day since your first trip to

Concord, full of remorse, begging me to help him convince you that he didn't mean to hurt you."

"What does talking to you do for me?"

"First of all, he needs someone to talk to and I'm his closest friend. The fact that you're my sister has made it more difficult…"

"I'm sorry that you're being dragged into this."

"No. Don't feel that way. Besides, it's certainly been a wake-up call for me where Maria is concerned. She and I have talked every night about being willing to share everything, no matter how difficult it may be. And, oddly enough, our relationship has gotten stronger. To think it took your marriage problems for me to make changes in my relationship with Maria."

"I'm glad someone is getting something positive out of this mess," Carolyn said ruefully.

Brad gave her a sad smile. "I'm certain that Lucas wants to win you back. And you know how convincing he can be when he wants something. All I can say for sure is that you have to be prepared to forgive him. Otherwise, your marriage is over. If you can't forgive him, you can't move on. The shadow of what he did will hang over you and Lucas for good. If he can't convince you that he's sincere, and you can't let go of your suspicions, there's little hope."

"Oh, Brad, don't say that." There was a solid ache around her heart. Her throat felt parched. "How do I get past feeling so betrayed by him? And there are times when I wonder if there were other women. I worry I'm a bigger fool than I thought."

"Carolyn, if only you could see Lucas when we go on the road together. It's a traveler's nightmare. I've shared a room with him, heard stories from other engineers who've traveled with him. He's either going full-out, talking up a storm or fast asleep. We've nicknamed him the Whirling

Dervish. Take my advice. Do not go on a business trip with him."

He gave her a sappy look that had her throwing her head back and laughing for the first time in weeks. It felt wonderful. "You are so good for me. I have this image of you trying to go to dinner in some city and Lucas insisting on working the entire dinner."

"I swear. Some nights I would insist on pizza delivered to the room, just to get a break while he went out to dinner with colleagues or clients. But he would always return so fast I wondered if he'd simply inhaled his food and left the others at the table."

His expression turned more serious. "Carolyn, I'm hoping you can forgive him, as I don't want to face down another brother-in-law. And I read somewhere that women usually pick the same kind of man. And with my luck, there's another Lucas out there somewhere." He grinned at her. "Just kidding, but you get my point, don't you?"

"I do." She leaned into his shoulder feeling a little better. "I'm so happy you found Maria. I really like her."

"Whoops." He peeked at his watch, pulling his cell phone off his belt. "I was supposed to call her after I talked to you. I hope you don't mind, but I'm not staying the night here. There's a beautiful woman who is more than able to say what she needs. And she needs me."

She waved him away. "Thanks for being here. Go and have a good evening. I'm fine."

"What are you going to do?" he asked before leaving a message for Maria to call him back.

"I'm going to have a long soak in the tub and think about what you said. Maybe I can't forgive him." she said, her throat tightening.

"Don't say that, please," Brad said. "You will work this out. The entire office is rooting for you."

"Stop it. You're not taking me seriously," she grouched.

He took her shoulders in his powerful hands and looked straight into her eyes. "You are going to find a way to talk to Lucas, or Maria and I will hold an intervention with the two of you. I'm serious. You have to work this out."

An hour later, she was about to settle into the tub when her cell phone rang. Lucas. At first, she wanted to let it go to voice mail, but the old need to hear his voice won out.

"How are you?" he asked when she answered.

"I'm okay, I guess."

"Carolyn, I realize you're angry at me and with good reason. But I was listening to you when you said we needed to arranged things for Summer and how she fits into our lives. I'm going to try and work from here for a week or so while Summer gets really comfortable with me, rather than coming home right away. In the meantime, I wondered if you and I could talk on Skype."

She thought about it. Despite her anger and disappointment over his behavior, she couldn't resist a chance to see him while they talked. "I would like that."

"Would you like to do it now?" he asked, his excitement clear in his voice.

"I'd need to go to the house and get the computer. I'm at Lucas's condo."

"I can wait," he said softly, his voice intimate.

"Okay. I was about to take a bath, but it can wait."

"No. I don't want to rush you about this, and I know how much you love soaking in the tub. Why don't you call me when you're at the house and on your computer?"

"I will. See you in about an hour," she said, a smile edging along her lips.

Excited and upbeat, Carolyn drove over to her house, took a shower, blew her hair dry and put on makeup. Touching up her lipstick, she felt as if she were going out on a date with Lucas, rather than simply talking on Skype.

Settling in front of the computer in the home office, she dialed Lucas's Skype number, startled by how quickly his face appeared on the screen. "You look great," he said.

He seemed anxious, his eyes searching her face. "You, too." She smiled at his compliment.

"So, what do you want to talk about?" she asked as she searched his face.

"Ah... I... You're right. We do need to work a few things out around when I bring Summer home. I've thought about what you said. I'm not putting our personal problems on the back burner while I stay here. We can talk like this after Summer is in bed." He cleared his throat nervously. "I... What do you think?"

She would have preferred that they talk in person, but given the circumstances, she was willing to compromise. "I agree. We need to put together a plan for Summer. How's she doing?"

"She seems okay, but I'm not sure. I have no idea how to recognize the symptoms of emotional distress, and I don't want to do something that would cause her any permanent damage." His concern was evident on his face. "I wonder if we should hire a child psychologist for her. At least to do an assessment. What do you think?"

Realizing that he was asking for her advice, she impulsively touched the screen. "I think that might be a good idea. Neither of us knows enough about grief in children. We need all the help we can get. What does Lisa say?"

"I haven't really asked her that question, as I feel it's our decision to make." He smiled at her, lifting her heart. "Do you have any other ideas on what we need to do to help Summer?"

"You could ask her kindergarten teacher how she's doing.

Other than Lisa, that's someone who would know if there has been a change in her behavior."

"That's a great idea. Why didn't I think of that? Or Lisa, for that matter. I'll arrange to meet with the teacher and see what she says... I miss you."

"I miss you, too," Carolyn said, a yearning for him and their life together sweeping through her.

After a few minutes of staring at each other through the screen, Lucas asked, "What are you planning to do until I get back? I mean, are you planning to stay at Lucas's?"

"Sorry to bother you," a voice broke in.

Lucas turned away from the camera. "What is it, Lisa?"

"A parcel arrived for you from your office," she said, passing a large brown envelope to Lucas.

"Where are you, Lucas?" Carolyn asked.

He faced the screen, a small frown on his face. "I'm in Deidre's home office. It's a great workspace. See?" Lucas panned the room for her.

Carolyn studied the background, the framed photos of Deidre and Summer, searching for any pictures of Lucas as her pulse pounded in her throat. "You're working out of Deidre's office?"

He shrugged. "It just made sense to stay here to be near Summer. There's almost everything I need right here." He turned the envelope over in his hands. "And this looks like the documents I need for the Perlman Project."

She wasn't sure why Lucas being in that room was so upsetting, but it was. It felt...wrong to her. "You're in her office," she said.

"It's just easier and we're so busy at work these days. And finding workspace downtown on short notice is difficult." He looked at her. "Oh, Honey, I didn't think about how this would feel for you. I just saw the opportunity to be near Summer while I worked."

"I feel as if you and Summer are settled there, all comfortable, thanks to Deidre. I don't feel good about you working in her office, around all her personal things. It's enough that you're living in her house."

Lucas closed his eyes, took a deep breath. "I didn't mean to cause you any pain. But we're in a difficult situation, and we need to fix it as best we can. I don't know what else to say."

"I don't, either. I know I'm partly responsible for all this, but it's hard for me to see you there in Deidre's home. And right now, I'm too worked up and too tired to do anything about it. I'm going back to Brad's condo. Talk later," she said, closing her computer.

CHAPTER THIRTEEN

As the days dragged on with Lucas still away, Carolyn felt aimless and at odds with everything around her. She'd cleaned her brother's condo from top to bottom, watched daytime television, something she never did. The days still continued to drag by. She and Lucas talked every evening, but he was always so full of stories about Summer.

In a way, it was a relief to have him out of town as it gave her time to think about her life, and what she wanted. She missed him, but there was a distance between them that hadn't been there before. She hoped it was simply living in separate places, but she wasn't sure. And it scared her. She had loved Lucas for so long, and he'd been part of her life since high school, leaving a huge open space in her life that she didn't know how to fill.

During their calls back and forth, they'd decided that he would bring Summer to their house two days from now, and she'd done nothing at the house to prepare for that. She would get groceries and change the beds. But Lisa and Lucas would have to move the crib already set up in the room intended for the baby they were going to adopt.

Tears stung her eyes at the thought of how excited she'd been putting the baby's room together, but that was all over now. She needed to concentrate on today. There were things she needed to do to get ready for their arrival. And despite her misgivings, she wanted the move to go well.

Once at the house, she made her way around to the garden in the back. The sweet scent of lavender greeted her, filling her with a sense of calm. The garden was her design and her effort that had converted an ordinary backyard into a flowered space that her neighbors and friends praised. She enjoyed their compliments and freely shared gardening tips with anyone who asked. As she glanced around she spotted a brown rabbit near the hedge, his nose twitching in curiosity. She waited to see if he'd come closer. Instead, he turned and hoped away deeper into the hedge.

She recalled the day Lucas had hurt his shoulder moving the lumber into place for her raised beds, the day he nearly stumbled carrying an armload of sod to fix the ground around the Koi pond in the center of the garden. She remembered rubbing his sore muscles with an anti-inflammatory cream to ease the pain. She also remembered the lovemaking after they'd showered together that day.

How had they come to this place where they had trouble talking to each other and no longer shared even the simplest things?

She longed for those innocent years when everything seemed to go their way, when trying to get pregnant was fun, not reduced to an anxious endeavor, fraught with insecurity.

She glanced around her garden, taking it all in, remembering each shrub and plant she'd lovingly planted. This space soothed her soul, warmed her heart. She hoped Summer would like it. As she looked around the space she realized that she needed was to get her hands dirty, feel the soil on her fingers and enjoy the results of her hard work.

She walked the stone pathway leading to the rear of the garden, then opened the garden shed and went in to the dark, moist space in search of her gloves, a spade and a rake.

The first area in serious need of her attention was the herb garden. The rosemary had developed long scraggly branches and the cilantro was suffering from lack of water. Getting into a rhythm of digging and weeding, the smell of the earth and the wind sighing in the Maple tree overhead, made her feel in control, able to cope.

She'd been working diligently, feeling the sense of accomplishment she always did as she cleaned up and weeded a garden area. She glanced at her watch. Whoops! She needed to get back to the condo. She wasn't sure what time Lucas and Lisa would be getting to the house, but she didn't want to be here when they arrived.

Scooping up her tools, she headed to the shed. Just then, she spotted the rabbit hopping in front of the trumpet creeper, a climbing shrub that clearly needed to be trimmed, but not today.

Back in Concord, Lucas and Lisa loaded his rental car, then placed Summer's car seat in the back. "Thanks for all your help," he said, trying to wedge the trunk of the SUV closed. "I had no idea how much gear a child needed. And that car seat was complicated to install."

"Get used to it," Lisa said, laughing as she turned toward the house. "I'll put Summer in the seat for you."

"Thanks," he said as he checked for the keys and linked his cell phone to the online system in the car. He had to call Brad as soon as he could. Working in Deidre's office was okay, but not the same as being where he had everything, files and paperwork, at his fingertips. Thanks to Brad and one of the other engineers, he'd managed to put out a few fires, but a lot of work was still pending.

He'd make some phone calls on the drive while Summer slept. At least, he assumed she would sleep. She'd awakened at four o'clock, crying for her mother. He was exhausted but he'd sleep when he got home.

Summer and Lisa came out of the house, Summer hugging her black bear. He opened the back door. "In here, sweetie," he said, feeling upbeat and ready to take his daughter home where she belonged.

The only thing missing was Carolyn, and the fact that she was living in Brad's condo. He had to believe that with time she would change her mind about being part of Summer's life. She loved their home and her life there. There were certainly things they needed to work out, but he wouldn't let himself believe that she wouldn't be willing to be part of his life.

She needed time and he would give it to her.

When he got Summer and Lisa settled, he would convince Carolyn to meet him somewhere, maybe for coffee or dinner. He had to convince Carolyn to come home.

Summer stomped down the driveway to the back door of the SUV, her bear crushed against her chest. She stopped. "No! I want to go with Lisa."

"Summer, I explained that you and I are going to travel with you dad."

"No!" Summer screamed, racing toward the house and crying at the top of her lungs. "I want Mommy! Mommy!"

He started toward her, but Lisa touched his arm to hold him back. "I'll get her. You stay here," she ordered before walking up the driveway.

Summer's tears felt like a physical blow, and he was powerless in the face of her unhappiness. He waited while

Lisa knelt in front of Summer and talked soothingly to her. In a few minutes, Lisa returned holding Summer's hand.

"What do we do now?" he asked Lisa, trying to remain calm. "I suppose we could always put the seat in your car."

"Not a good idea. Your car is bigger and safer. Besides, it will take even more effort to change the seat. I think it's best if we simply go," Lisa said.

Summer stood next to Lisa, her tiny shoulders shaking, her face buried in her bear's neck. "I want Mommy," she sobbed over and over.

Lucas could barely breathe over the anxiety knotting his chest. His heart hurt for his little girl but he didn't know what to do to help her.

"Summer, you and I are moving to your new home with your daddy. I need you to get in his car. I'll be driving my car right behind you. Whenever you want, you can get your daddy to call me on his cell phone and you can talk to me. How's that?"

Summer looked up at him, her tear-stained face wrenching his heart. He had to convince her that she was to go with him, all the while fearful that he'd made a horrible mistake in insisting on moving home. "Summer, if you'll go with me, I promise you that we will stop at a McDonald's and a park on the way so you can have fun on the trip. It isn't just about going to my place. It's about having fun along the way, isn't it? And Blackie would like to go on a set of swings and eat in a restaurant, wouldn't he?" Lucas asked, feeling an overwhelming sense of relief when his daughter looked up at him.

"McDonald's has toys," Summer said, hugging her bear close, the beginning of a smile forming on her face.

"Well done," Lisa whispered as she helped him get Summer into her car seat. "You're catching on fast."

The drive proved he hadn't caught on all that fast.

Summer talked, hummed or cried all the way. The only break Lucas got to make calls was at the rest stops and standing outside in the rain at a McDonald's. Completely exhausted when he got home, he was pathetically grateful when Lisa offered to unpack the car and settle Summer in her new room.

He was grateful to find that Carolyn had gone for groceries and everything needed to make dinner; potatoes, carrots, chicken fingers and salad. "Summer is up in her new room putting her books on the shelf. That room is ready for a baby. You'll have to take the crib down and put up her bed before bedtime. I assume you have a single bed some-where...or I could put her in one of the other bedrooms for tonight."

Memories rushed him. The hours his wife had spent painting the room, the bookshelves they'd scoured antiques shops looking for, the hours spent huddled over wallpaper samples. All of it for a baby they'd never had. He choked back his sorrow, seeking to answer as normally as possible. "I'll put the twin beds back and take the crib out."

Lisa gave him a sad smile. "You can tell me to mind my business, but in a way, this is my business because of Summer. You need to make amends where Carolyn is concerned. You can't go on living like this. And neither can Carolyn."

"She didn't want to be here. I have to respect that."

"Maybe for now. But you have to make things right with your wife," Lisa said.

He looked at her in surprise.

"I mean it," she said. "You two need to work on your marriage and stop being so defensive with each other."

"I hear you. It's just been so confusing. We seem to be constantly on edge with each other."

"No wonder. Anybody would be under the circumstances."

"I'm going to call her right now and see if she will meet me somewhere, anywhere we can talk."

He picked up the phone and dialed Carolyn's number. When it continued to ring, he started to worry. As his call went to voice mail, he left a short message saying they were home. Yet, after their last call when she'd been so unhappy, he began to wonder if she might have decided to see a divorce lawyer.

Carolyn was about to settle in front of the TV when her cell phone rang. Lucas. Undecided as to whether she wanted to talk to him, she let it ring. After he'd made several calls she decided to pick up.

"Carolyn, we're here at last. Thanks for getting the groceries."

"You're welcome."

"How are you doing?" he asked.

"I'm fine. Brad's away for a couple of days."

"I miss you, so much," he said.

"I miss you, but you must be really busy with the move." She heard screaming in the background. "Sounds like you have your hands full."

He sighed. "Yeah, we got in about an hour ago. Summer's exhausted from the drive, and to be honest, so am I. She cried, sang or talked the entire way. My ears are hurting. Seriously."

"There's a lot that needs to be done to get her settled."

Oh, how she wanted to rush home to help him! But she couldn't. Lucas needed to take responsibility for his decisions. She had always stepped, smoothed his life for him. But not this time. "Have you looked into kindergarten for her?"

"Haven't even started that. I should have made a few calls last week, but it's been hectic."

"I can imagine," she said, reveling just a little in the idea that Lucas was experiencing the results of doing little or no planning before bringing Summer here. It was probably mean of her, but she couldn't help how she felt. If he'd listened to her in the first place, none of this would have happened.

"Maybe I can drop over sometime."

"That would be great. I'd love to see you. This house isn't the same without you. When would you like to come? What about this evening?" he said eagerly, and for a moment, she felt the old closeness.

And despite everything that had happened and all her negative feelings toward him, hearing the sweetness in his voice she gave in. "Why don't I drop over when Summer's in bed?"

"Come over anytime. Really. Lisa is great with Summer, and I'm sure we could find a quiet place to talk," he said, over another loud scream.

"I'll see you later," she said, aware that she was in danger of doing whatever he wanted of her. She hung up quickly before she fell for the intimate tone, the enthusiastic response and said the words he wanted to hear. Lucas had always been so enthusiastic about everything going on in their lives, his boyish spirit and drive being two of the main reasons she'd fallen in love with him.

In the quiet of Brad's condo, she faced her thoughts. She loved Lucas. She needed him. But she couldn't continue feeling left out, of little importance except to do as he wanted and fulfill his needs. She wished she could believe in him again. But the man she'd married was rapidly disappearing behind his plans, his dreams, his obsession. Not hers. And not theirs.

A bit later, she pulled into the driveway.

Lucas met her at the door. "I've been waiting for you," he said, his words punctuated by Summer's yelling about not wanting to go to bed.

After an earsplitting shriek, he said, "She wouldn't eat her supper, and we don't know what to do with her," he said apologetically.

Carolyn saw the strained look on his face and the bags under his eyes. "You're still getting unpacked, I assume," she said, wanting to touch his cheek, to massage the worried frown on his handsome face, to feel the smoothness of his skin.

"Trying to," he said just as Summer came running down the hall toward the door.

She stopped. Her red curls bounced around her head. "Who are you?" she asked as she put her thumb in her mouth and stared at Carolyn, smudges of tears evident on her cheeks.

"I'm Carolyn," she said, unable to keep the smile off her face. With her bright blue eyes, and curious expression, Summer was a charming little girl.

"Do you live here?" Summer said.

"I..." She didn't know what to say.

Summer pursed her lips and scowled. "What do you want?" Summer asked, speaking around the thumb in her mouth.

"I came to visit."

Stepping around Lucas, Summer held her hand out and looked into Carolyn's eyes. The sudden sense of connection charged through Carolyn like an electric current.

"Want to see my teddy bears?" Summer tugged on Carolyn's hand.

"I'd love that."

"Let's go."

"She loves to show people her bears," he said, a wry smile on his face as he led the way to the stairs.

Carolyn exchanged a quick look with Lucas. "Are you feeling a little overwhelmed?" she asked.

Lucas rubbed his jaw. "Summer isn't happy with me or Lisa right now. She hasn't eaten anything since we got home."

"Summer, I haven't eaten, either. Maybe you and I could have a peanut butter sandwich together. What do you think?"

Summer smiled as she headed up the stairs, her pudgy hands gripping the handrail as she took the steps one at a time with Carolyn following.

"Want to see my room? My bears are in here." Summer pointed.

Carolyn hesitated. It was the room that held all her hopes and dreams for a child of her own. And now another child, her husband's child, occupied the space Carolyn had imagined spending time in, rocking her baby, watching her child fall asleep after reading her or him a story.

Could she go in there and not break down in tears? She didn't know, but she had a little girl waiting for her answer... "Show me your bears."

Summer grabbed Carolyn's hand and pulled her to the door, her fingers warm against Carolyn's skin. "See. These are all my teddy bears. I love bears. Do you?"

Her heart sank at the changes in the room. The crib was gone, and in its place a single bed stood between two dressers. The bed had been hastily made up. The mobile that had hung over her baby's crib was dangling off the end of the bookshelf. Her throat ached with loss and regret.

"Are you crying?" Summer asked, her voice gentle and oddly quiet as she tugged on Carolyn's hand. "Mommy says that tears are needed sometimes." She slipped her thumb into her mouth, then pressed her face into Carolyn's leg. "I want Mommy," she said, her voice breaking.

Carolyn scooped Summer into her arms and sat on the edge of her bed, rocking her back and forth to ease the little girl's distress, while she tried not to cry herself. "Your mommy was right. Tears are very needed sometimes, aren't they?" she asked, still holding the child, feeling the warmth of her little body.

She held Summer as emotions long kept in check flooded over her. The powerful connection created by soothing and caring for such a precious little girl left her suspended in a place where only she and the child existed. This was what she'd waited for all her life, the touch of a child. Her child.

She stroked Summer's head soothingly, letting her snuggle. In this moment, she and Summer had a bond. They'd both lost a part of their lives they'd wanted. Summer had lost her mother. Carolyn would never give birth to a child. Smoothing Summer's brow, Carolyn whispered into her curls, "Summer, this room was decorated for a little girl just like you."

Summer leaned back in her arms. "Like me?" she asked, a quizzical expression on her face.

"Yes. Your dad and I wanted a baby just like you."

"Did you have one?" Summer whispered, her eyes wide ovals of deep blue.

"No. We didn't. But now you're here," Carolyn said, looking directly into the toddler's eyes, feeling a sudden sense of finding something for the very first time.

"I'm staying here," Summer said.

"You are. For sure."

"Will you be here?"

She didn't know how to answer Summer, but in her heart, she knew that more than anything she wanted to be here with this wonderful little person. "Would you like that?"

Summer's eyes darkened. "Lisa is here, but she's not staying very long," she said.

How does she know that? Has she heard a conversation between Lucas and Lisa?

"Summer, there will always be people who love you even when they can't be with you," Carolyn said, her heart pounding in dread. Summer had to be tired. And tired children could get upset very easily. She didn't want Summer to be afraid that she might be left alone by yet another person. How could Lisa even think about not staying here with this little girl? "Your dad loves you very much. He will always be here for you."

"My mommy's gone. She's in heaven with the angels," Summer said, a forlorn look on
her face.

"Yes, your mommy is with the angels and you can pray for her whenever you like. I'm certain she's looking down on you and loving you from heaven."

Summer gave a long sigh and snuggled closer.

Carolyn held Summer in her arms as gently and lovingly as she could, and decided that whatever it took, she would try to work out her differences with Lucas. Not just for Lucas or for her, but for this wonderful little girl so in need of love and reassurance. She kissed the top of Summer's head. "Why don't we go downstairs and I'll make you the best peanut butter sandwich you ever had."

"Better than Mommy's?" Summer asked, her face turned up to Carolyn's.

Looking into the child's eyes, she was reminded how fragile life could be. A car accident, a few seconds of distraction or misjudgment had forever altered this little girl's life. "No. Not better than your mommy's. Nobody could do it better than she did," Carolyn said as she took Summer's hand and led her down the stairs.

"No. Mommy's sandwiches were really, really. good," Summer said as she hopped down each step while still holding on to Carolyn's hand. It was a bumpy trip down the stairs, and when they reached the bottom, Lucas was waiting.

"Want to join us in the kitchen? I'm making peanut butter sandwiches for Summer and me," she said to him, watching his eyes search her face, warming her heart.

"I'll make them," Summer called out as she moved ahead of Carolyn.

"You know how to do that?" Carolyn asked, her eyes still focused on Lucas.

"Of course! Mommy showed me," Summer said proudly, her tiny chin tucked into her chest.

Carolyn and Lucas shrugged at each other. "Well, Carolyn, I guess it's time for us to see what sort of culinary skills Summer has," he said with a smile as they followed Summer down the hall toward the kitchen.

"She has cried ever since we got here, until you arrived. How did you do that?" he asked, his fingers brushing hers.

Carolyn looked into Lucas's eyes and recognized pain and uncertainty, eagerness and caring, all in his glance. She wanted to touch him, to tell him everything would be okay for Summer and for them.

But she knew it wasn't that simple. If they were to make any of this work, they needed to take it slow, not say things that might end up being worthless a few days or weeks from now. "She cried a little while we were in her room, and I let her. She needed to cry. She's missing her mom."

"And I can't figure out how to help her," he said, as they walked into the kitchen. His hand brushed hers again, sending an exciting thrill up her arm.

"Summer, your daddy's going to be your assistant and help you make the sandwiches. Is that okay?" Carolyn asked, at once pleased and a little sad to be entering her kitchen, the one she designed.

"What's an assistant?" Summer asked.

"It's the person who helps the person making a meal," Lucas said, smiling his thanks to Carolyn as he went to the cupboard to get out a loaf of bread.

"I do it," Summer said, taking the bread and pulling the fridge open. Reaching into the shelf on the door, she took out the peanut butter.

"Let me help you," Carolyn offered.

"Okay." Summer put her arms up to be lifted onto a bar stool at the kitchen island.

Carolyn got a knife out of a drawer. "Why don't you lay out the bread slices, Daddy, while I get the jam? Then you can help Summer put the peanut butter and jam on the slices."

"Sounds great," he said, helping Summer to spread the slices with a thick layer of peanut butter and jam.

At the sight of her husband being so caring to his daughter, she had to turn away to hide her tears. When she turned back, Lucas was watching her.

"Okay. Done." Summer patted a sandwich until peanut butter oozed out of it.

"I'll put the sandwiches on plates and take them to the table," Lucas said, his eyes still on Carolyn, making the heat rise in her cheeks. He took dishes from the shelf, his arm brushing against her as he moved around the kitchen.

"What does everyone want to drink?" he said. "If we were not being observed by the princess, I would kiss you right about now," he whispered, leaning closer as he opened the fridge.

"I want milk," Summer called from the table.

"What about you, Mrs. Turner?" Lucas said, continuing to whisper.

"Water is fine," Carolyn said, feeling the heat of his body, smelling the scent of his skin. She wished they were alone.

"Daddy!" Summer called. "I want milk!"

"Coming right up," he said, pouring a glass.

"This is the best," Summer said excitedly as she munched on her sandwich.

"You bet it is." Carolyn said, glancing around the kitchen, feeling connected and happy.

Lisa came into the kitchen. "I'm settled in my room. This is a lovely home."

"We've always loved it," Carolyn said, forcing back the memories of all the work that had gone into making this house their home. And the hours they spent making meals, dreaming of their child, and the disappointment they'd shared. Needing to escape the memories she finished her sandwich, got up from the table and knelt next to Summer. "See you later, alligator."

"After a while, crocodile," Summer said giggling.

"I can see myself out," she said, touching Summer's curls, feeling their softness, as Summer smiled at her.

Lucas came around the table. "I'll walk you to the door."

"Do you know when Brad will be back?" she asked, feeling awkward when they reached the door. Would he try to kiss her? If he did, what would she do?

"He should be here tomorrow," Lucas said, his eyes searching her face. "Carolyn, I would like a chance to talk to you. Can we meet somewhere tomorrow? Maybe for coffee?"

"That would be nice," she said, resisting the urge to move into his arms.

"Carolyn, you were fantastic with Summer. Thank you."

"You're welcome." She pushed the strap of her purse up her shoulder.

Lucas shifted from one foot to the other, jamming his hands in his pockets as he did so. "I just want to say that I'm so sorry we never had a baby together. You're a fantastic parent. All this time you waited to do something that comes so easily and naturally to you. I can only imagine how painful it has been."

The expression on his face, the way his eyes searched hers made her see that he was sincere. She wanted to reach out to him, to touch him, to show her appreciation for his saying that, but she couldn't. If she did, she'd cry, and she'd cried enough these past few weeks, endless days of wishing things had been different in their lives and in their marriage. "I'd better go."

"Can I call you tomorrow?" he asked as she opened the front door.

"Yeah. That would be good." She didn't look back as she went down the walkway. She couldn't. If she did, she would surely run to him, into his arms, to the life she'd lived as his wife.

But that would mean she'd have to give up on her belief that he had to change, that he had to be willing to really listen to her. Being the one to relent, give in over an argument, had always been her style. She'd always taken the first step after any disagreement they'd ever had. She couldn't this time. There was too much at stake, too much of who she was, who she believed herself to be, to be the one who offered to reconcile their differences.

She opened the car door, climbed in and drove off into the darkness.

CHAPTER FOURTEEN

Lucas called the next morning just moments after Carolyn had gotten out of bed. "It was great to see you yesterday. And I wondered if you might be available for coffee or tea this morning. I could bring coffee over if you'd like that."

Stifling a yawn, she said, "Don't you think it's a little early? I just got up."

"You never sleep in. Feeling all right?" he asked, concern evident in his tone.

She wasn't about to tell him that she'd lain awake for hours last night, missing him lying beside her, reaching for him knowing he wasn't there. Waking up to an empty condo with no one to talk to, to share things with, had been heart wrenching. It all felt so awful. She didn't want to live like this. "I'm fine. I slept in a little bit, that's all."

He gave a low chuckle. "I've got the perfect fix for sleepiness. Will we go out for coffee or will I bring it over to the condo?"

"Why don't you come over here?"

"Great. I'll bring coffee and your favorite banana muffin and be there in a few minutes. Can't wait to see you, Carolyn," he said, his voice thick.

"Me, too," she said before hanging up.

She rushed through a shower and was about to apply a little blush and eye shadow when the doorbell rang. "I'm coming," she called out as she strode toward the door. When she opened it, Lucas stood there holding a bouquet of her favorite yellow roses and a cardboard carrier with two coffees and a bag of muffins.

"Carolyn Turner, I want this to be our first date of our new life together," he said, passing her the roses.

She took the flowers as her eyes met his. "It's been a while since we had a first date."

"Sixteen years, four months and thirteen days, to be exact," he said, following her to the kitchen.

"You have a better memory than I do," she said, putting the roses in a vase and adding water, all the while delighted that he'd remembered so well.

"I wanted to impress you, so I did the math and counted up the time. We met when we were sixteen. We've been together half our lives."

"Leave it to the engineer to figure that out," she said.

"Carolyn, I know I'm repeating myself, but I've missed you. I can't live like this anymore. You have to come home. Please."

She wanted him to cross the kitchen floor and kiss her senseless, but she knew if he did, she would give in and move home with nothing being resolved. As much as she wanted her husband, she couldn't go back to the way it was.

"First we have to talk, really talk, about what has gone on in the past few weeks." She took the coffee and muffins to the table.

"Anything." He sat across from her, took the lid off her coffee and slid it across to her before opening the bag and passing her a muffin with a napkin. "First, I'd just like to say how much I appreciated you coming over last night. Lisa and I were at our wits' end. And the peanut-butter thing was pure genius. Summer asked where you were when she was having her bath and went to bed without a tear."

He took a sip of his coffee. "Summer got up this morning and was her old sweet self. Of course, yesterday was a difficult day for her. I should have realized that it was too much, but I really felt that getting back here was the best answer."

"I know you did," she said, remembering the many times they'd have coffee just like this before he went to work.

"I really messed up when I didn't talk to you about what we should do. I was so focused on helping Summer that I lost sight of what was really going on between us."

Was he finally going to talk about all of that? She felt her body relax in relief. "You left me out completely. Even though you were aware that all of this was a shock to me, that my belief in us as a couple was shaken to the core, you didn't get the fact that I felt abandoned while you and your daughter came first."

"I get that now. But how do I fix it?"

"Tell me why you got involved with Deidre," she said, clasping her hands tightly in her lap, her coffee cooling in front of her, her stomach threatening to reject the bite of muffin she'd swallowed.

Lucas looked up at the ceiling, then back at her. "I doubt you realized what was really going on when we started trying for a baby. Our every moment together was taken over with having sex at the right time, whether or not you were pregnant, whether or not there was a physical reason why we couldn't have a baby. I felt as if I was a cog in a wheel, a person whose only function was to produce enough sperm at the allotted time to get you pregnant. It was awful."

"Why didn't you say anything?"

"I tried to a couple of times, but you always seemed so preoccupied, I felt as if you weren't listening. There never seemed to be a time when we could stop and look at what we were doing to each other. The three years we were married before we started getting involved in fertility testing, when we thought we could have a child easily were good, but then when we realized that we had to seek help everything changed. We didn't go anywhere together except for some appointment or other. Instead of holding you in my arms and talking about you and me, and how much we loved each other, we talked about when you'd probably ovulate again. I knew the inside of the fertility clinic waiting room in more detail than I did our living room."

"I've never heard you talk like this before. I had no idea that you felt so...pressured by all of it."

"Didn't you feel that way?" he asked.

"At times, yes. But I believed, in the end, we'd have a child."

"Well, that's where you and I saw it differently. The longer it went on, the less I believed that we'd succeed. I'm not blaming anyone or anything. I just didn't feel the whole thing was going to work, and I didn't know how to say that without upsetting you."

"So you went away on business, saw an opportunity..."

"Carolyn, don't say it like that. I was...confused...lonely. The time I spent with Deidre was wrong and I felt terrible about it, but she listened to me." He looked across the table at her, his eyes dark, his face pale. "And as stupid as that sounds now, I needed someone to hear me."

Carolyn searched his face. He was telling her the truth. A truth she didn't want to hear. Had she been so unaware of him and what he needed? "I thought you were as involved as I was in getting pregnant. You mean you weren't."

He shook his head slowly. "I didn't know how to tell you."

"All those months you went along with trying for a child because you felt you couldn't disappoint me?"

"I did. You were so much more committed than I was. I began to think that I didn't want it as much as you did. You talked about it all the time. I wanted to have the old Carolyn back. The one who liked to spend a morning reading the papers in bed, having sex simply for the fun of it, going for a walk without checking the clock or talking about the latest test results."

"I had no idea you were so unhappy."

"It wasn't that I was unhappy. I felt guilty that we hadn't had a child. I wanted you to have everything. I'm your husband. I wanted you to be happy, and I knew how much a baby meant to you. I felt inadequate seeing you so anxious."

He reached across the table, his fingers touching hers. "I don't want to dwell on the past. We have a bright future ahead of us. I want to resolve things so that we can be a family, you me and Summer," he said, his smile wrapping around her in a wave of love that left her breathless and her heart thudding against her throat.

They were all wonderful feelings, but they couldn't mask the hurt roaring through her at his admission. "Did you ever consider how hard trying to get pregnant was for me? Yes, I did want a baby more than you did, So you can imagine how painful it was for me to learn that, after a couple of nights with a virtual stranger, you were able to have a child with her, a woman you claim not to care about. And even worse, when you find out you had a daughter by this woman, you act as if the only people who matter are you and Summer. You make your plans without talking them over with me.

And I'm expected, as usual, to simply go along with what you want."

"And that was a mistake on my part. I want to change how I do things. From here on, we will talk through things, and you will see that I'm serious about taking your feelings into account."

"I...I want things to work out between us. I do," she said.

"I never meant to hurt you. You don't believe that right now, but it's true. I didn't mean to leave you out, but there was a little girl, and I was responsible for her."

"And you had a wife who had just gotten the shock of her life when she learned that her husband had had a child by a woman he hardly knew. You never once asked me what I needed, how badly I was feeling or what I thought we should do. You were bringing your child into our marriage without ever consulting me on how we should do it," she said, her voice rising.

He rubbed his hands through his hair. "Carolyn, those first couple days were so overwhelming. I was so anxious to see that Summer was taken care of."

"But she had a nanny who was perfectly capable of caring for her."

"I see that, now." He gave her a wry smile, emphasizing his dimples.

"Lucas, taking on a child is something we've never done. It was supposed to be you and me facing the arrival of a child in our lives. And you left me out of every part of it, until now."

Lucas met his wife's anxious gaze. That this conversation was painful for her was evident in the hurt and uncertainty he saw in her eyes. His heart thudded in his chest. He felt as if he'd betrayed her all over again and it broke his heart.

Fighting to remain cool and in charge, he thought of all those times they'd sat across from each other in the school library, studying, laughing together, sharing the same jokes and loving the same things. It was as if they'd been born for each other. He'd never felt that way about anyone in his life. Never, in all his wildest dreams, had he imagined anything but the blissful happiness they'd experienced from the first time they'd locked eyes on each other.

"All I want is to care for you and Summer. If you're willing to help me, I swear, I'll make it up to you."

"If I believe you, and I want to..." She played with the edge of her coffee cup, her eyes focused intently on him. "How do we do this? How do we start over? Where do we go from here?"

"I'm not sure. All I am sure of is that I don't want to make any more plans without you involved." Their old connection, the intimacy they'd always shared, rolled over him. There would never be anyone for him but her, and it was time he put it all on the line. "Carolyn, would you like to go on a date with me?"

"What?" she asked, her eyes wide with surprise.

"We can't figure out how to move forward, or at least, I can't. I'm beginning to see that I've not only hurt you over everything I did, but I haven't been treating you like my wife. I have taken you for granted. Sure, I can come up with reasons, but they'd probably only sound like excuses to you. The fact is, you've always been there for me, and I've always assumed you would be."

Her hands stilled on the cup. "What did you have in mind for a date?"

Where would be the best place to go to dinner? Some place she loved. "I'll make reservations for Dominique's and pick you up. We'll have a wonderful evening together. Just the two of us. We won't talk about anything going on in our lives. We'll simply enjoy each other's company. I'd like to start new, go out on dates. Then, once we're both feeling more at ease with each other, we can move on to planning our future together. What do you think?"

Thrilled by his words, Carolyn wanted to lean across the table, run her fingers through her husband's hair and kiss his lips. His words of explanation touched her deeply. That he'd shared his feelings over the fertility testing, his shame over what he'd done, made it possible for her to see his actions and choices a little differently.

Maybe there was a new way to approach this. It might not be a perfect way to resolve their issues, but if they went back to where they had started, their attraction to each other, their caring, they might have a chance to rebuild the trust between them. "I accept your invitation to dinner, but I'll drive."

His wide smile filled her heart with desire. There had never been a time in their marriage when she didn't want him to make love to her, making what he'd done even more painful. But she would work on moving ahead, starting over.

"Why do you want to drive?"

If she drove, she could control what happened after the dinner. As much as she cared about him, the date could not be about making love. She was well aware what would happen if she allowed it. He'd kiss her, hold her and the rest would be inevitable.

She was not going to let that happen because she needed to believe he was truly changing and not just doing this to get her to agree to whatever he wanted to do about Summer.

She needed to be convinced that he was genuinely interested in her as a woman, a partner. Her confidence had taken a beating after the revelation of his affair and Summer's existence. Carolyn needed to be assured that he respected her as well as loved her. Nothing less would do.

"Lucas, if we're going to do this, it has to be on my terms. We're in this mess because of your behavior." She clasped her hands in her lap to keep from reaching for him. "We've lived for all these years thinking we knew each other. Maybe we don't. It's time we found out," she said.

"I'm all for that. What time are you picking me up?" he asked, a smile spreading across his handsome face.

CHAPTER FIFTEEN

Carolyn applied lipstick, her hand shaking so much she was afraid of smudging it. She'd spent the entire day getting ready for their date, including buying a new dress in shades of green and gold that fit her body like a glove. She'd never owned a dress like this one, but it was going to be part of her new image.

After applying a bit of blush to her pale cheeks and putting gloss on over her lipstick before checking her face one more time in the mirror, she put her makeup away. Standing in front of the full-length mirror, she smiled at her reflection. She felt so good, pleasure bubbled through her. She hadn't been this excited in years. She remembered her first date with Lucas. They went with a group of friends to the movies where they'd shared popcorn and tried to make conversation.

"Maria and I are here waiting in the living room to see you off on your date," Brad said, coming down the hall toward the bathroom. "Ready or not, we want to see how you look."

She opened the door and stepped out into the hall. Lucas

gave a long, slow whistle. "Sis, you look spectacular," he said, pulling her close. "Lucas won't know what hit him." He led her to the living room. "Maria, what do you think? Is my sister not the most beautiful sister in the world?"

Maria strode across the room to hug her. "That dress is perfect on you. One very sexy dress. I don't think I've ever seen you in anything so sexy," she said.

Maria's job as fashion coordinator for the local department store meant that she always dressed well, another trait Carolyn admired about her. "If you like it, then I'm good to go," Carolyn said.

"The only thing I'd add is a smoky tone to your eye make-up," Maria said, heading toward the bathroom. Quickly and with complete confidence, she applied the shadow to Carolyn's lids. "Lucas is one lucky man. That's all I can say."

Maria's gaze met Carolyn's in the mirror. "I think Lucas needs his butt kicked for the way he's behaved. I mean, he had everything and he tossed it for a hookup. Men. Sometimes I wonder..."

"You're not wondering about Brad are you?" Carolyn asked.

"No! But before Brad I was involved with someone who didn't tell me that he'd had an affair on the side. I was so hurt and angry. I had invested my total self in the relationship only to find out that he'd been with someone else."

Carolyn touched Maria's arm. "I'm so sorry."

"Thanks. It was really messy at the time, but when I realized that he was the one who made the mistake, not me, that I was the excuse he used to justify what he did, I got angry. And getting angry saved me from slipping back into those patterns of thought." She gave her forehead a gentle smack. "Sometimes I wonder what we women use for brains when it comes to men."

What had happened to her had happened to someone

strong and amazing like Maria. "You're right. This isn't my fault at all. I wasn't the one who broke our marriage vows."

"That's the attitude, girl. You just remember that you deserve a man who knows how to treat a woman. Someone like your brother," she said, winking. "And if Lucas doesn't come to his senses and behave like a loving husband, he'll have my man to deal with."

"How serious are you and Brad?" Carolyn asked.

Maria nodded her head slowly, a smile lighting up her face. "Very serious."

"Oh! That's great!"

"Isn't it? I'm excited. He's asked me to go looking for a diamond with him, but I'm a little more traditional. I'd like him to pick something he likes. As for me, it's not about the diamond. It's about our future together."

"I couldn't agree more. It's not about the ring. It's about the love and the future together. I can't wait to have you as my sister-in-law."

"And we're both taking it slow, getting used to being with each other, to sharing our lives, our interests." Maria glanced at her watch. "You'd better get a move on. You're going to be late picking Lucas up. By the way, I think it's totally cool that you're driving, shows him you're in charge."

"I hope so." Carolyn hugged Maria, went to find her evening bag, kissed her brother's cheek, then headed for the door. "Love you. See you both later."

"I guess I can't ruffle your hair the way I did when we were kids," Brad said.

"Not a chance. After all the work Maria and I have put into this." She flicked her hands down her body. "You *cannot* touch my hair."

. . .

The traffic was light and Carolyn got to the house earlier than she expected. She thought about slipping in the back door, but decided to come to the front instead. Like a real date. A scream of delight greeted Carolyn as Lisa answered the door. Summer peeked out around Lisa's leg, her thumb slipping into her mouth, a smile of welcome on her tiny, upturned face. Unable to resist the little girl with the mischievous grin, Carolyn knelt down. "Hello, Summer. What's up?"

Summer pulled her thumb out of her mouth. "I'm playing with my Barbie doll. Do you want to play with me?" she asked, stretching out her hand.

"I would like that very much."

"Lucas's been on the phone for the past hour," Lisa said. "He just now headed upstairs to get dressed."

Summer tugged on Carolyn's hand. "Come on. I've got lots of dolls," she said. The soft touch of the little girl's skin filled Carolyn with happiness. As they entered the kitchen, she stopped. Everywhere she looked, there were toys. The TV was turned to a Thomas the Tank Engine program. The late-afternoon sun streamed over the counter where a little pink sweater dangled from the corner.

This was exactly how she'd imagined her kitchen would look when she and Lucas had children of their own. She'd imagined making breakfast while her toddler played, Lucas coming downstairs, scooping up their child and squeezing in between her and the island to kiss the nape of her neck. She'd imagined so many wonderful moments. Moments that had never come true. She swallowed over the lump in her throat. "I didn't realize that four-year-olds played with Barbie dolls," Carolyn said.

"Her mother bought a lot of toys, from dump trucks to Barbie dolls, and let Summer make the choice of which to play with."

"Wanna see my dump trucks?" Summer asked still holding Carolyn's hand. "Or we can sit at my table and have tea." Summer pulled Carolyn to the child-size wooden table and chairs near the window. "Please, Lisa, can we have tea? Just the three of us. And Daddy, too." She popped her thumb back into her mouth as her gaze moved to the door leading to the hall. Summer had clearly begun to feel at ease around him. The idea warmed Carolyn.

She was suddenly overwhelmed with caring and concern for this little girl who had been through so much and still faced the loss of her nanny when Lisa went back to Concord. How would Summer cope with her dad at work and Lisa gone? Carolyn couldn't imagine what it would be like to be so young and face so many changes in her life.

"I would love tea," Carolyn said, kneeling next to Summer's table, patting her narrow shoulders as Summer moved the dishes around in a businesslike fashion.

"We have to get tea for Sam and Pedro, Barbie, Ken and Tammy," Summer said.

"Is everyone having tea?' Carolyn asked, loving this moment of make-believe.

"Oh," Summer said, her lips rounded and her eyes bright with anticipation. "Do you want to make a peanut butter sandwich? Like we did the last time? All my dolls like peanut butter."

"That sounds like fun." The way Summer's eyes widened when she was excited about something was so cute.

Lisa wiped her hands on a towel, folding it neatly. "Summer, honey, you've already had your dinner. We need to get you ready for bed. Besides, Carolyn is here to pick up your daddy."

Summer's lower lip trembled. "Are you taking my daddy away?"

How difficult it must be for Summer to understand what

is happening in her life. To think that she would fear someone taking her daddy away broke Carolyn's heart. She hugged Summer, smoothing the curls from her face and looking into her anxious eyes. "No. Never. No one is going to take your daddy from you. I'm going out to dinner with him so we can talk."

"About me?" Summer asked, leaning closer to Carolyn as she played with the gold necklace she was wearing.

"A little bit, maybe," she answered honestly. She saw the downcast look in Summer's eyes, and wanted to hold on to her forever. "Do you mind?"

Summer snuggled closer to Carolyn. "Has my mommy really gone to be with the angels?"

"Yes. Your mommy's in heaven with the angels."

"How do you know?" Summer asked, her dark eyes wide in question.

"I just know. Someone who loved you so much would definitely be in heaven," Carolyn said.

Suddenly it came to her: What if she'd said the wrong thing? What if Lisa or Lucas had given Summer a different explanation? She glanced hurriedly at Lisa, to see her nodding slowly.

As she held the little girl, feeling connected to her, imagining what it would have been like to hold her own baby. What would it have been like to give birth to a wonderful little girl just like Summer?

She sensed someone standing behind her. Glancing up she saw Lucas, a happy expression on his face.

"Summer needed a little comforting," she offered, the words hung suspended between them. She searched for a way to express her feelings, the changes this child had wrought. Changes that went so deep they rocked Carolyn's belief in herself.

He knelt beside her. "You are so good with Summer," he

said, his eyes dark with awareness as his hand touched her shoulder.

For the longest minute, she wanted him to take her in his arms and kiss her breathless, show her how much he cared by making love to her. It took all her willpower not to act on her feelings. "I think it's time we got to the restaurant," she said, holding back the loving, bittersweet emotions his touch sparked.

"Whatever you say," he offered, taking Summer in his arms and brushing the curls off her face. "Summer, Daddy's going out with Carolyn, but I'll be back." He kissed her round cheeks, making her laugh, a beautiful sound that tugged on Carolyn's heart.

Still in her father's arms, Summer reached for Carolyn. "Hug. I want a hug."

Stepping closer to Lucas, Carolyn kissed Summer's cheek and, in doing so, breathed in the cologne she'd given Lucas for Christmas. She felt light-headed at the nearness of him, the possibilities of the evening ahead. "Good night, Summer."

"Good night," Summer said, giving Carolyn a big, noisy kiss and a smile as she waved.

It took every bit of determination to move away, out of Lucas's reach. She wanted to touch him, to feel his skin, soak in his scent, but it was too dangerous. She had to keep her head clear, focus on working out the issues between them.

"Summer, it's time for bed. Say good night," Lisa said as she took Summer from Lucas.

"Night, princess," Lucas said, kissing Summer before handing her to Lisa. "I'll be back real soon."

"And in the meantime, Summer will have her bath and I'll read her a story," Lisa said.

She wanted to be part of Lucas's life and Summer's. Everything she'd ever wanted and everything she stood to lose was in this house. Quietly, she went to the door. He must not see her tears. He would want an explanation and she couldn't give him one without admitting how much she loved him and wanted their life together back.

Once outside, Lucas took her hand in his. "That dress is so...so sexy," he said, his words, easy, seductive.

"You like it?" she asked, fighting the urge to press her body to his.

"Let's put it this way. I have a date with the sexiest woman I know."

Fighting her desire, she led the way to her car, letting her hips sway beneath the shimmering fabric. At the restaurant they listened as the waiter told them a humorous story about his eight-year-old son learning to play the violin, while they ordered their favorite food. When the meal arrived, they talked and ate as if nothing was wrong between them. "Do you remember the first time we saw a movie together?" Lucas asked.

"Yes...Miss Congeniality. An old movie. Benjamin Bratt and Sandra Bullock. We laughed all the way through it."

"And how many times have you watched since?"

"Probably three or four times," she said, loving how it felt to have his full attention.

"I've never known anyone who enjoys watching reruns of movies like you do." He picked up his wineglass. The old connection, so strong between them even after all these years, came alive. It was as if they'd never been apart, as if none of the events of the past weeks had happened.

She smoothed her hair, her fingers touching the necklace at her throat. "How's work going?" she asked to keep the conversation on a safe topic.

"Busy." Lucas sighed, putting his wineglass down. "In fact, we are going to exceed our profit projections for this year based on the first six months."

He continued to talk, giving Carolyn a glimpse into the

business that excited him. She'd always loved his passion for his work, even though she didn't understand most of what he did. Yet, she had always supported him, and he never failed to appreciate everything she did...until now. Which is why his behavior was so unexpected and so painful.

"Sorry. I tend to talk too much about business." He leaned back in his chair, glancing around for a waiter. "What would you like for dessert?"

"Not tonight," she said.

"Are you sure? What about lemon gelato? It's your favorite."

"Not tonight. This dress is really tight," she said, resisting the urge to pull it down a bit. "I don't think I could move if I ate one morsel more."

"I've got an idea. Let's drive out to the each and watch the waves. We always loved doing that," he said.

His suggestion called to mind the days when they had no money and went to the ice cream shop near the pier. More bittersweet memories. Still, a walk on the beach would be pleasant and distracting. "Why not?"

"Will I drive?" he asked.

"Why would you want to drive my car? Aren't you the one who claims that it drives like a grocery cart?" she asked, slipping easily into their teasing banter.

"I'm doing my good deed for the day by saving all the oncoming traffic from my wife, the centerline hugger."

"While Mario Andretti, here, thinks that the speed limit is for turtles," she said, laughing for the first time this evening.

He shifted in his chair, his smile warm, his gaze intense. "You look gorgeous," he said. "I love the sound of your laughter, the way your nose crinkles when you grin."

'I love you' was on her lips, but she held back. Her laughter was one of the first things he'd complimented her on when they'd started dating, and something he never failed to remark on. Funny, how he'd always been able to make her laugh. And she'd always said she loved him when he did; a habit honed from years of loving the same man.

They arranged to take coffee with them, then headed out onto the highway to the beach, the windows down, the air ripe with scents of tidal water and muddy inlets. The street leading to the beach was lined with shops selling trinkets, and restaurants with patrons spilling onto the sidewalk.

"I love this," Lucas said as he pulled into the parking lot next to the pier.

"It's certainly busy tonight," Carolyn said as she watched him maneuver her car into a narrow parking place.

"Do you want to take our coffees out to the boardwalk?" he asked, turning off the engine. "Or let's have coffee on the bench over there." He pointed.

They settled on the bench, sipping their coffees as they watched the people milling around.

"This is so nice, just sitting here, the moonlight on the water, being with you," he said.

"It is. I wish…"

"What do you wish?"

"That things had happened differently. That we had been able to work things out, not have it go so wrong," she said.

He slipped his arm around her shoulders as they moved closer to each other. "I would give anything to go back to that moment at the Parker House Inn. To start over, to say the things I should have said, not the things I did. I rushed everything when I should have taken it slow, let you take the lead. I didn't. And you'll never know how sorry I am for all of it."

His eyes meeting hers, he said, "If it would change how you feel about me, I would be willing to move Summer and Lisa back while we sort things out between us."

"You can't do that to Summer. She's been through enough, from losing her mother to losing her home."

His expression was bleak as he held her closer, his forehead pressed to hers. "But I can't live without you."

"But we have so much to work out between us, if we're ever going to get back to the way it was."

"Isn't that what we're doing now?" he asked, touching her cheek, sending waves of desire spiraling through her.

Lucas stroked her cheek. "Carolyn, you mean everything to me," he whispered, touching her cheek, eliciting a sigh of need.

As his dark eyes searched hers, he kissed each finger slowly and deliberately. "I want to make love to you all night. I want your skin on mine, our bodies together." He nibbled on her lip, his mouth hot against hers.

She sank into his embrace, her head spinning, her body angling closer to his. He smoothed her face, his breath warm, his eyes on her lips. "Carolyn, please," he breathed.

She fought for air, her heart tumbling in her chest. She wanted him, his skin, his body, his words, everything. As his gaze, simmering with passion, met hers, she faltered.

"Lucas, we can't do this," she said, seeking to put a little space between them.

He moved away, while keeping her hand in his. "Carolyn, we need to find our way back to each other. We need to trust each other, work together. We need that now more than any other time," he said, his deep baritone voice playing over her, toying with her resolve.

"Lucas, what we need is for each of us to put the other first. I can't make love to you, not yet. When you're close to me, I can't stop myself from imagining you holding another woman."

"That was five years ago, Carolyn," he said, disappointment seeping through his words.

"Not for me," she said. "I found out only a few weeks ago, so for me it feels as if it happened yesterday."

He eased away from her. "I don't want you to feel pressured," he said. "I meant for us to simply spend the evening with each other. No expectations."

Glancing down the beach, he said, "Let's go into the hotel and have a drink. Maybe reminisce a little." He took her hand and tucked it against his body.

She matched his stride as they walked. "I can't remember the last time I was inside that hotel," she said, allowing the moonlight to chase away her disturbing thoughts.

"The last time I was in this hotel was when we came here for dinner to celebrate our new office space. Do you remember that?" he asked.

"I do," she said, matching his carefree tone, even though she wasn't feeling very carefree. She felt lost, out of touch with her life, somehow. Lucas was everything to her, but he had a new priority in his life, one she wanted to share.

"One of our first dates was at this beach, having hot dogs at the little takeout on the pier. That was one of the most memorable dates we had. I was so sure I'd blow it and you'd go off with Peter Woods and I'd be left holding the beach bag."

"You're kidding. Me and Peter Woods? Never," she said playfully. "He wasn't after me. He was after Sue Beck. Remember her?"

"Yeah. How I remember her...all that black hair," he said, glancing at her out of the corner of his eye, a smile teetering on his lips.

"You told me you didn't like her."

"I didn't, really. Wonder what we'll find when we get to the bar. Probably a bunch of people staring at their cell phones."

"And, of course, you've never stared at your phone," she said, giving him a gentle poke in the ribs.

He laughed, pulled her close and kissed her. "Guilty..." His gaze caught hers, held her...and then he slowly looked away. "You can't imagine the fantasy playing in my mind at the moment. You. Me. Our big four-poster bed..."

Struggling to recover from the force of his kiss, she said way too quickly, "I wonder if they've redecorated since we were here last."

He took her hand and pulled her along with him. "I hope so. It wasn't a very attractive bar back then."

They entered the lobby of the hotel and went into the wide-open space of the bar. Taking a table by the window, they sat in deep, comfortable chairs across from each other, their hands touching casually.

She glanced around. The color scheme had changed from taupe and grays to mostly black and turquoise with splashes of white and cream. The room was filled with small tables along the windowed area, while the bar with high stools and tables occupied the rest of the space.

She liked the way they'd opened the bar up to be part of the lobby area. Young couples and singles milled about. "New color scheme."

"Different crowd. They seem a lot younger than I remember," Lucas said.

"And you might be showing your age," she teased. "I remember when we were in our twenties, when everything seemed possible."

They ordered wine and continued to people watch. "This must be a popular bar by the size of the crowd."

"We were here to a wedding reception once and there was a dance floor over there." She pointed to the back of the room near the entrance. "I wonder if they ever have dances here."

"No. This is probably a bar for hookups. People coming on vacation looking for a quick fling. I hear my staff talking about how dating works today. Were you aware that there are apps you can get for your phone that allows you to find someone to hook up with on a moment's notice?"

Is that what you did? Did you and Deidre hook up in a bar like this one?

He said that they'd been working, but what if they went to a bar for a drink after work? She couldn't stop the sudden rush of images. Her husband touching another woman, kissing her in public...laughing...sharing a joke. Deidre flirting with him, making it clear she wanted him. No strings attached. Just sex...

She felt the blood drain from her face. "How do you know about that?" she asked, her voice sounding distant, not part of her body.

Surprise dawned on Lucas's face. "Because of some of the younger people I work with."

"Is this how you and Deidre got together? Did you go to a bar?"

"No! We worked long hours together..." He rubbed his face with his hands, his eyes bleak as he met her desolate gaze. "Look, I never hang around bars when I'm out of town. They don't have any appeal for me. I eat in the dining room of the hotel, then head upstairs to work. I've always done that."

"Except when you hooked up with Deidre," she said, aware of how angry and judgmental she sounded, but she didn't care. Seeing these people behaving in such a casual way, enjoying themselves, some of them probably cheating on their partners made her want to throw up.

"Carolyn, look at me," Lucas said, taking her hand in his. "I've never been in a bar like this without you. I swear."

She stared at him, at the man she thought she'd known, for so long. "But you did have a relationship."

Lucas put his hands in his lap, his face impassive, his tone quiet and controlled. "I've told you how it happened."

"How do I know that what you're saying is the truth? Look around. Whether innocent or not, these people are here for something besides a drink."

"I swear to you. It only happened that one time, Carolyn," he said, his gaze searching the room as he took a deep breath. "I'm sorry I brought you here if it reminds you of what happened. I'm truly sorry," he said, defeat in his voice. "I think we should leave."

Numbed, she followed him out to the car, her heart breaking. But she couldn't help lashing out. And even worse, she was still so angry at him, at what he'd done and how it had destroyed her happiness. When they reached the car she slid into the seat, despair filling her.

Lucas climbed into the driver's seat. "Carolyn, we have to resolve this somehow." He gripped the wheel and stared straight ahead. "You are my life. I want you to be with me and with Summer. I want you to be part of everything we do. But if you and I can't get past your fears...pain...what then?" he asked, his voice haggard.

"I just can't believe that someone as caring as you are would have casual sex, Lucas. It's not like you. That's the part I can't accept."

"You're right, it's not like me at all. That's my whole point. It was a one-time thing."

"You say that, but I find it so hard to accept that you could be so indifferent about something so intimate. It makes me feel inadequate, as if I wasn't enough for you."

She swallowed against the futility of it all. This shouldn't be happening. She longed for the days when they were excited and hopeful about having a baby, rather than this. This awful, hurtful experience that had destroyed her self-confidence and her trust in her husband. "Regardless of how you felt about everything going on with us and your work, why did you do something so hurtful to me, to our marriage?"

Lucas sighed. "I don't know, Carolyn. I was lonely and working long, hard hours with her, eating in her office. We were together and suddenly... I... Things were all mixed-up in my head. It was a long time ago," he murmured, pain and hurt flowing through his words.

She stared across the small space separating them and felt as if she were looking at a stranger. She didn't know this man nearly as well as she thought she did, and it frightened her. "I don't know, either."

His gaze met hers, his face drained of any emotion. "I'm out of ideas, Carolyn. Please help me figure out what to do."

Carolyn felt sick. The marriage she'd put her whole life into felt like a sham. Something she'd imagined, or wanted so bad, she'd created. "I have no idea." Sadness wrapped around her heart, crushing her spirit. "I really have no idea how we're going to work this out."

"You know what frightens me the most?"

"What?" The desperation in his eyes made her fear his answer.

How she wished she'd never said what she'd said. It only made more trouble for them to deal with, adding to their problems, and maybe for no reason if he was telling the truth. And if he wasn't, there was nothing she could do to alter the past and the hurt they'd both experienced, widening the gulf between them.

"I'm scared we can't fix this. That you will never forgive me for what I did. That Summer and I will live our lives without you. I wish things were good between us, the way they were. We were happy together, regardless of what happened these past few weeks. You have to admit that." He pulled out of the parking lot. "I'll take you to Brad's place, and bring your car back in the morning.

CHAPTER SIXTEEN

As Lucas drove back to Brad's condo, he struggled to think of something to say that would give him an opening, an opportunity to make one last try. She was still upset, and he didn't blame her for that, but if they were to ever to get together again she had to help him find a way he could make it up to her.

He'd been glancing her way every couple of minutes, but she didn't look at him. He wanted to pull over to try to reason with her, but hadn't dared to do that, fearing that he'd only make things worse. All he could do now was encourage her to call him tomorrow. He didn't feel he could call her under the circumstances.

When he pulled into the entrance to Brad's condo building, his brother-in-law was walking toward the door. He retraced his steps when he spotted Carolyn's car. "Hey, Sis. You're back early," he said, a quizzical frown on his face.

"I'll explain later," she said, not looking Lucas's way. She picked up her purse and got out. "I'm really tired," she said, hugging her brother.

"Talk to you tomorrow?" Lucas asked, aware that his

brother-in-law would have a long talk with Carolyn tonight or tomorrow, then Brad would call, demanding to talk to him.

Carolyn didn't turn back, didn't make eye contact or smile. "I'm sorry for tonight," he said, hoping she'd at least say good night.

Lucas got into the passenger seat Carolyn had just vacated. "Okay, buddy, what did you do to my sister?"

"It didn't go well," Lucas said, feeling defeated.

"If you don't make this right, you need your head read," Lucas said, giving Lucas's shoulder a light punch. "The last thing I expected was to have her show up looking like she'd been hit by something."

Lucas stared in surprise. "I would never.'"

"Relax. I know you wouldn't. But you are messing up badly. What's going on?"

"I don't know. She won't listen to me. I'm going to lose her, Brad. And I can't seem to turn this around. I need your help."

"You got it. But first, I want to check on Carolyn. Maybe I can get a handle on what's happening with her. I might be able to sit down with you tomorrow if I can get out of going to Nashville again."

Lucas's heart sank at the stiff expression on Brad's face. He'd offered to help, but would he if he thought there had been other women besides Deidre? "Brad, I didn't have any other relationships. Deidre was the only one. I swear to you. Man-to-man. I never, ever, intended to do what I did. You have to believe me. I wouldn't intentionally hurt Carolyn."

"I don't have an answer for you. Only that you've got to fix this, one way or the other." Brad got out of the car. "I think you should face facts. If you don't put your wife first, you're going to lose her."

. . .

Carolyn leaned on Brad for support as they went into the building. "You'll be all right, Sis, really," Brad said as he pressed the elevator button. "I'm getting you upstairs, then we're going to have a talk about what's going on with you and Lucas."

"Please. No lectures. Not tonight. I'm too tired." She leaned against the wall of the elevator as the stress of the evening washed over her. She could still feel Lucas's body pressed to hers, his mouth on hers, desire for his touch flooding her senses.

"I'm not going to lecture you, but you need to sort this out. I'd like to kick his butt, but it wouldn't do much good. Lucas can be a brick-head when it comes to personal connections. But this isn't news to you, right?"

"Yeah," she said, her whole body feeling lethargic, her mind in complete turmoil.

Brad touched her shoulder. "Don't mean to be hard on you, Sis, but there has to be a way to get this settled. I've never known two people who loved each other the way you two do."

"Maybe it was all just a sham," she said.

"You don't believe that. Not for a minute."

"No. Lucas and I had everything but a baby. I want to believe that if we'd been able to have a child, this wouldn't have happened. But I'll never know, always be left wondering if wanting to have a baby so much ruined my marriage."

"Do not believe that. Do not," he said emphatically.

"I may not have a choice."

"You can't change the past, and don't go blaming yourself. Lucas was the one who made the mistake."

She walked ahead of him from the elevator, down the hall toward his condo. "What do you mean?"

"Let's go inside first."

"Is Maria here?"

"No, she' s doing email at work this evening."

"I really like her, Brad. Are you going to propose to her?"

He tilted his head at her. "We are not discussing my love life. We're discussing yours. I'll make us a hot chocolate like Mom used to make. Remember how good that tasted? The ultimate comfort food."

Whenever they'd needed a little cheering up, their mom would get out the saucepan to make real hot chocolate, none of those just-add-water packages. "Yeah. I miss her so much, and even more now with my life in such a mess."

Brad busied himself mixing the ingredients together, the scrape of the spoon on the pan the only sound. He turned the burner on under the saucepan. "Sis, honestly, I don't have a clue how I'd feel in your shoes. Wanting a baby, then finding out that Lucas had a child by another woman."

"Brad, can we not go there tonight?" She pushed her hair off her face, irrationally feeling Lucas's skin against hers when he'd kissed her.

"Sorry. I didn't mean to start there, but we have to start somewhere. You need to decide what you want to do about it."

"Like what?" she asked.

"Well, if you and Lucas aren't going to settle your differences, then you'll need to look for somewhere to live. It would make sense for you to stay at the house, but he'll have to move his daughter somewhere, another move for the little girl. Not the best choice. Or you could find a condo or an apartment while you get to work on your divorce."

"Divorce! I don't want to divorce Lucas."

Slowly Brad turned with the saucepan in his hands, filling two mugs with the steaming brown liquid. "If you don't want to divorce him, what do you want?"

"I want Lucas to understand that he's hurt me, and I need time to get over it."

"Then maybe you should simply get an apartment while you decide if you're ready to forgive him or not."

"You make it sound like I'm punishing him."

"Aren't you?" Lucas cocked one eyebrow at her.

"No! I'm the one being punished. I'm the one who has to find a way to live around my husband's infidelity."

"Carolyn, that was five years ago. Five years during which you've been happy, right?"

"Yes...except for not having a baby."

"And then you got the letter..."

"Yes. And right after that the phone call about Deidre."

"A rough time for both of you."

"Yes. But he has to stop making all the decisions for us, for me."

Brad gave her a look she knew well. "Okay. Out with it. Why are you looking at me like that?" she asked.

Lucas put his cup down. "Carolyn, if you want your marriage, I suggest that you get over there and talk to your husband about Summer, about what you want out of life. Get the ball rolling."

"It's not that simple," she said, feeling defensive, something she rarely experienced around her brother.

"It is, if you love him. If you don't love him, then get out of his life. He's my brother-in-law and I'm mad as hell at him for what he did to you. But he's also my friend and my partner. In all the years I've known Lucas, he has been an honorable man who loves you. I've envied him that happiness. As I've gotten closer to Maria, I've learned something that is key to loving someone. You have to talk to each other, no matter how painful the subject is, no matter how difficult or even embarrassing it is to share how you're feeling. If you love someone, you talk, you listen."

"We've been talking," she said, wishing this conversation could be over.

"Have you been listening? Seriously listening?"

"I'm very aware of how Lucas feels about all that has happened," she said remembering how emphatic Lucas was about his responsibility to Summer.

"Then you heard how unhappy he is. How he's willing to do whatever you want if you'll come back."

She couldn't deny that. "Yes."

"And despite knowing that your husband is ready to do whatever it takes to win you back, you're still willing to throw all of that away because you can't forgive him."

Brad took Carolyn by the hand and led her to the sofa. "Your husband, the man you love, made a mistake in judgment five years ago. If you can't listen to him, understand his side of things, and find a way to accept his mistake, you need to move on and let him go."

She stared at her brother as his words hit home. "You think Lucas and I are headed for divorce?"

"I have no idea. All I know is that you need to face the reality that if you can't find common ground, a way to settle your differences, you may end up facing the very real possibility your marriage is over. Lucas loves you and he loves his daughter. If you cannot accept that and become part of it, you could end up living without him."

Brad tucked her hand in his. "You've always wanted to be a mom. I realize that this wasn't the way you'd imagined you'd become one. And although it is a little unorthodox, you have a little girl in your life who needs a mother."

An ache started under her rib cage, slowly moved toward her heart. "What if it's too late for that? I mean, Lucas and I don't seem to be able to figure this out. Nothing is going right between us. What if he feels forced to choose between Summer and me?"

"Don't let that happen. I'm the one person who has been around since the beginning of your relationship back in high school. You two were meant to be together."

CHAPTER SEVENTEEN

Lucas had driven home in her car, and the next morning he had Lisa follow him while he dropped Carolyn's car off, leaving the keys at the desk in the condo building. She hadn't called since.

He couldn't stop thinking about what Brad had said. His brother-in-law hadn't been able to get out of his Nashville commitments, so their talk had been postponed. Lucas understood better than anyone why Brad had to go, that he couldn't ask someone else to head up the meeting on a project that would see them break into the Nashville market.

He'd called work this morning to let them know he wouldn't be in. He had several large files, pricing reports and some new project proposals he needed to review, and his home office was the quietest place he knew, provided Lisa could manage Summer.

But he was home for another reason. He needed time to think. He had left messages for Carolyn. And there had been no response. She was making it clear she didn't want to talk to him, and he had nowhere left to turn...unless Brad could help. But Brad was busy, and he couldn't expect him to solve his problems with Carolyn.

He'd been thinking of ways to restart the conversation with his wife. They'd always loved going to Hilton Head for a break when his work allowed. Maybe if he took Carolyn away to for a few days without any outside interference, he might get a conversation going again, show her that he had changed, that her opinion mattered.

But that might not work given how much he had to do in the next weeks. He didn't want to promise her a trip away, only to disappoint her. With everything else going on, he still had to find a good kindergarten for Summer. He had two recommendations from staff at the office, and he had an appointment with each of them before the weekend. But he could send Lisa in his place if he managed to get Carolyn to consider a trip.

He was about to open his computer and start his workday when Lisa came downstairs into the kitchen. "Lucas, while Summer is playing in her room, I have to talk to you."

Lucas's heart jumped into his throat. "Is it about Summer? Is she all right? She's not sick, is she?"

"No. Summer's doing really well. I'm truly amazed at how easily she's settled in here. It's me I need to talk to you about. I've been offered a job in Concord. It's full-time, looking after twin boys. It will mean I'll be near my mother and able to care for her when needed. The pay and accommodations are good. The only problem is they want me on the job by the end of the month."

That was a little over two weeks away. He'd planned on Lisa being here for another month, at least. "That sounds like the perfect job for you."

She glanced at the pile of paperwork, then at him. "I hate to leave you so soon, and Summer is still missing her mom so much. But I feel that I need to take this position. Losing Deidre and watching Summer grieve has been very hard on me. I had always believed that I would be with them until Summer went to high school. They were as much a part of my family as my brothers and sisters, but that's all changed now."

"I understand. You've been through a lot."

"And you, too. I truly believe you will work things out with your wife. She's a lovely person and Summer adores her. For me, an offer like this won't come my way again, and I do need to be near my mother."

"It's not going to be easy to replace you, Lisa. I wouldn't have been able to manage without you these past few weeks. But of course, you have to do what's best for you. I'll start looking for someone right away."

"Thanks, Mr. Turner. I hope that you get your issues resolved with your wife. She is a natural when it comes to children. Summer is always asking when she's coming to the house."

"Thanks for saying that. There is nothing I'd like better than to have my wife back here with Summer and me."

Lisa touched his arm consolingly. "You'll figure it out. Over the next week I'll stock up on supplies of food and things that Summer will need, regardless of who is caring for her. And I will visit those kindergartens, then give you my evaluation, if you like. I know what to look for where Summer is concerned. I helped Deidre pick the one in Concord."

"Thanks, Lisa," Lucas said with regret. "We'll have to tell Summer together."

"I dread that the most. She'll be so upset, and will I be too. How do you think we should do this? How do I tell my little girl I'm leaving her?" Lisa asked, biting her lip and turning away.

With a loud clatter, Summer arrived at the bottom of the stairs. The both went to check on her.

"Oops! My dump truck fell. Just fell. Like that." She flipped her hands open and shrugged her tiny shoulders in a show of disbelief.

"Summer, you're going to put your dump truck in the toy box, aren't you?"

"Yep. When are we going to the grocery store?" Summer asked. "We need more peanut butter. And I want more cheese but no yogurt. Yogurt is yucky," she said as she wandered into the kitchen, chatting all the way.

"When will we tell her?" Lisa murmured.

"I'm not sure," Lucas said.

"I'll miss her so much," Lisa said with a catch in her voice.

"And she'll miss you."

Lisa nodded as she smoothed her cheeks, removing the remnants of tears.

They followed Summer to the kitchen. She crouched in the middle of the room, focused on arranging several of her trucks and her tractor. "I'm building a house today. That's why I got to dig a giant hole in the ground." She looked over her shoulder at them, then went to Lisa. "Why are you crying?"

"I'm not."

Summer planted her hands on her hips. "You are, too."

Lisa ruffled the red curls forming a halo around Summer's head. "We have to get ready to go shopping."

"What are we buying?" Summer asked, smiling up at Lisa. "I love to shop."

"Spoken like a woman," Lucas said. How was he going to tell Summer that Lisa would be leaving them? And who could come to help him on such short notice?

Carolyn sprang immediately to mind, but he shied away from the idea. She would likely feel he was using her, further reinforcing her feelings of being left out of any decisions being made.

Lisa gathered the grocery list and her car keys. "Let's get your jacket and we'll head out. Where did you leave it, Summer?" she asked.

Summer swung around. Her lips pursed in thought, she turned all the way around one more time and pointed to the back of a chair in the dining room. "There it is."

"Then get it on. I need to speak to your dad for a minute, so you wait in the hall for me, okay?"

"Sure." Summer ran for her jacket. Pulling it on, she rushed for the door leading to the garage. "We'll play dump trucks when I get back," she said, dropping the one she held in the toy box behind her.

With Summer out of the room, Lucas turned to Lisa. "We have to tell Summer as soon as possible. We need to give her time to adjust to your leaving."

Lisa's eyes swam with tears. "Maybe I could wait and take another job. That way it would be easier on everyone. My biggest concern is my mother. She doesn't seem to be doing as well as the doctors suggested she would. It's all such a worry," she said, glancing furtively to where Summer was playing.

Lucas wanted Lisa to change her plans and stay longer. With more time, he'd have a better chance of finding someone with Lisa's skills. All sorts of scenarios went thought his mind at once. But he had to face facts: Lisa had the right to take a new job. It was up to him to find a solution as soon as possible. Otherwise, Summer would be even more unhappy and he'd find himself working from home indefinitely.

Abruptly he stopped and looked around. He was doing it again, making decisions for everyone. He'd done it to Carolyn without a thought. Slowly he reconsidered what he'd been about to do. He didn't need to take charge of Lisa's problems. He wasn't responsible for her. He needed to provide for his daughter.

"Lisa, I've not considered what it must be like for you, losing your friend and now having to give up a child you love as if she were your own."

"I am going to be so lonesome for her, but she belongs here with you. That's what Deidre wanted. I have to confess that I was pretty concerned when you wanted to bring her here so soon after her mom's passing, but she is settling in well."

Awkwardly, he patted her shoulder. "You do whatever you need to do. We will manage. And maybe you could come back to see us? You're welcome here any time."

"I'd like that," she said, taking a tissue from her pocket. "I'd like that a lot."

"Talking to Summer isn't going to be easy. Should we try for this evening?"

Lisa frowned. "I don't think so. She's usually so tired at the end of her day, which makes her really fussy. It might be better to talk tomorrow morning. She's going to be upset enough. No point in adding to it by timing it badly."

"Okay. Let's plan on after breakfast tomorrow. I'll call and let them know I won't be in the office tomorrow. I feel pretty sure that she'll need reassurance from both of us."

Lisa met his gaze. "Lucas, you're a good dad and a good person." She picked up her purse. "If there's anything I can do to make things right between you and your wife, I'd be willing to do it. It was pretty clear that first day I met her that she was hurt and shocked by what she'd learned. I feel guilty about the way I brought up the photo of you because it hurt her, something I didn't mean to do."

"You were pretty upset yourself, Lisa. We all made mistakes in those first few days."

With a sad heart, he watched Lisa and Summer go down the driveway. He felt empty and alone. He had so much to consider. First, he had to talk to Summer about Lisa leaving. Then he had to find someone to take over the house and care for Summer while he was at work.

He waited until Lisa's car had turned onto the next street before he turned to the job at hand. He called his office, asking his assistant to see if she could help in the search for a new nanny, then put a call in to the two kindergartens to move the appointments up so that he and Lisa could go together.

He was concerned about how tomorrow would go, how upset Summer would be to learn Lisa was leaving. The chaos underscored his need to have Carolyn here, especially while he talked to Summer. Carolyn would know what to say, how to handle this. Summer liked Carolyn. She was so strong. So capable of seeing what was possible, what would work best for Summer.

He'd been sitting staring at his computer screen, trying to deal with the paperwork spread out around him. But all he wanted to do was see Carolyn, a futile wish, given that she hadn't returned his calls.

He was still thinking of Carolyn when the phone rang. With trepidation, he answered, "Hi. What's up, Brad?"

"You are, you silly bastard," Brad said. "Like I promised, I'm coming over to your house. Put the coffee on," he ordered.

Whoa. Lucas's tone showed he was angry, which meant that Carolyn was, as well. But if he could reach Carolyn by having it out with Brad, he'd do it. "Okay. See you in a few minutes."

"You got it," Brad said before hanging up.

When Brad arrived, a scowl dominated his features like a

cloud before a downpour. "Coffee's on," Lucas said, taking two mugs from the cupboard. "Two creams?"

"Yep." Brad took the cup, had a quick sip, then leveled a look at Lucas he'd never seen before. "When are you going to fix things with my sister?"

"I've tried. She is still very angry about everything."

"And that's your excuse? Hell, Lucas, you can do better than that."

"Brad, she won't talk to me. Ever since we stopped in at the hotel bar on the beach the other night. She acted really strange and I could tell she was upset with being in the bar, being around singles... Or I assume that's what it was." Lucas put his cup down. "And I made a really dumb remark that didn't help things."

"Acting dumb is going around like a flu bug, it seems."

"Why do you say that?"

"I talked to Carolyn."

"What did she say?"

Brad sipped his coffee, a glum expression on his face. "Not much."

"That doesn't surprise me. Carolyn is still convinced that my relationship with Deidre went on a lot longer than it did."

"Did it?" Brad asked, his gaze fixed on Lucas.

"No!"

"Then get your act together. Carolyn is hurt over what you did. That's influencing everything for her."

Lucas nodded slowly as Brad's words cut into him. "What the hell am I going to do?" Lucas scrubbed his face, felt the stubble along his chin.

Brad nodded slowly. "Well, I can tell you that Carolyn's miserable. She sits in my condo and knits. She doesn't seem willing to talk to us, but something has to change. I just can't watch my sister being so unhappy and not do something about it."

"Brad, I had an idea last night, but can't do much about it if Carolyn won't talk to me."

"What's your idea?" Brad asked, a quick look of interest on his face.

"I thought I'd see if Carolyn would go away with me for a couple days. If we could find time alone, just the two of us, without any interruptions, maybe she could be persuaded to come home and try again with me."

Brad nodded as he eyed Lucas. "Okay, here's what I'm going to do. I'll talk to Maria and get her advice on how to convince Carolyn to see you."

Rubbing his jaw in thought, Lucas said, "Summer's nanny, Lisa, is leaving at the end of the month. She and I are going to talk to Summer tomorrow morning. What would you think if I asked Carolyn to be there? Am I being a total idiot to think she might be interested in being part of that?"

Brad stared at him for a few minutes. "I honestly don't know how she'd react. I'm pretty sure she likes Summer. In fact, my sister loves all children and wouldn't want to see any child hurt. I guess you could call her and see what she says."

"If you can get her to return my calls."

"Maybe the best answer is for you to go to my place and talk to her. Just give me fair warning you're coming so I can be out before you get there."

"I could give that a try. Would you be willing to give her a message?"

Brad scanned the ceiling before answering. "I'll put in a good word for you. I'm headed to the office and then out of town on the McLellan project. It's all up to you, buddy. Good luck."

Relief flowed through Lucas. "I'll try anything."

"By the way, if Carolyn is willing to go away with you, be sure to turn off your work cell. Nothing kills a romantic moment faster than a call from work." He tapped his chest. "I found out the hard way a couple weeks ago. I've never seen Maria more upset."

"And if I disappear for a couple of days, that will mean more work for you," Lucas said.

"All for a good cause. I need you to focus more on work, and Carolyn needs you back. Not to mention what Summer needs in all this."

Brad put his cup in the sink and slapped Lucas on the back before heading to the door. "Try not to blow it, Lucas."

CHAPTER EIGHTEEN

Carolyn sat alone in her brother's condo, trying to sort out her feelings. She'd hardly slept since her talk with Lucas. His words, his serious tone, had added to her fear that they wouldn't be able to work things out between them. Why did they keep getting it all wrong after years of getting it right?

Deep down she knew she'd been hiding out at her brother's place, knitting and watching TV. But she needed to do something to move on with her life, to figure out what she should do with her marriage.

Was Brad right? Was she simply unwilling to accept what Lucas said? That he'd made a mistake a long time ago, and it had nothing to do with his love for her?

And what about Summer? She couldn't help but love the little girl. Yet if she wasn't an equal partner in raising Summer and making decisions involving her, the rest of their relationship would suffer the consequences.

Yet, she missed Lucas so much, found herself thinking about him all the time. What was he doing? What was he feeling? Was he eating, looking after himself? Between his new family responsibilities and his work, he had to be under even more pressure.

She'd been at the table with Brad and Maria several times over the past days and heard how busy Lucas was, which meant that Lucas had even more work responsibilities than she'd known about. She wanted to call him, to let him know she was here if he needed her. But she couldn't get up the courage to do that, especially when she wasn't sure she could go back to the house and behave as if nothing happened.

But could she simply return his call? She touched the phone, her fingers tapping along its smooth surface. "Do it!" she said to the empty room.

She reached for the phone just as it rang. Caller ID showed Lucas's number. Suddenly nervous, she picked up. "Lucas?"

"Hi Carolyn, I'm working from home today, and I wondered if you might like to come over for coffee...or whatever," he said, his words tender in her ear.

Her body warmed at the memory of other times when he'd spoken to her like that. There had always been such warmth between them, such a powerful connection.

Her heart pounding in her throat, she clutched the phone, willing him to talk to her about how he loved her, needed her and wanted her in his life. He'd said it the other night, but in her anxiousness, she needed to hear it once more.

In that moment, she faced what had been uppermost in her heart. She wanted to be with him, to be part of what was going on in his life. Brad was right. She needed to believe what her husband said, or let him live his life without her. "What about now? Or maybe in an hour?"

"Come over now. I'm right here. I'll close up my computer and turn my cell phone off so we can talk," he said, his words coming fast.

"Okay. I'll be over in a few minutes," she said, her heart pounding in that old familiar way.

Carolyn drove carefully through the streets toward the house she loved and the man she'd married and had loved with all her heart. Did she still love him after all this, or was she simply wishing for her past life? Would he ever understand how much he'd hurt her? Despite how she felt about him, what he'd done five years ago would always be between them, influencing how they felt about each other; if they couldn't find a way to overcome it.

What if she got to the house only to learn that nothing had changed, that Lucas insisted on convincing her that she needed to see things his way? If he did, what would she do? She suddenly realized that she'd been placing all her hope in a meeting like this, one where they could share their concerns as a starting point. And if it didn't go that way...

As she pulled into the driveway, she noted that Lisa's car wasn't there. She had felt uncomfortable around the woman from the first moment she met her, mostly because Lisa seemed to know things about her husband.

Pushing her worried thoughts to the back of her mind, she got out of her car and went up the front walkway. The door opened and Lucas was standing there with a huge smile on his face, making her heart tumble in her chest.

He moved toward her...then stopped. "You're here." He sighed out the words. "Come on in. Do you want coffee?"

She glanced around at the smattering of toys lying about the front hall and the pink hoodie hanging on the newel post at the bottom of the stairs. "Is Summer here?" she asked, not wanting to have the little girl overhear their conversation.

"No. She's with Lisa, running errands." He smiled again, a smile so warm and inviting she wanted to walk into his arms.

"All of this feels so strange," she said, glancing around the living room, seeing the dollhouse at the end of the sofa and the Lego blocks on the coffee table.

The kitchen area was in disarray with the piles of files and the laptop on the counter, toys scattered everywhere. The sun caught the edge of the table where coloring books were spread out. Everything looked so lived in, so much the home of a child who was loved and cared for. "Summer must keep you busy."

"She does. She's basically taken over most of the house with all her stuff. And today I have a bunch of files that are in the way." He glanced at her anxiously. "Let's go to the living room. It's probably the least cluttered part of the house," he said, placing his hand in the small of her back, the heat of his fingers, the ease of his touch so familiar.

They faced each other, their eyes locked, the air between them charged with emotions that neither could express.

Finally, Lucas said, "Carolyn, I'm so glad you're here. I wanted to tell you how sorry I am that I messed up our date. I never considered that being in a bar would be so difficult for you and my thoughtless remark..." He glanced away. "I don't seem to get anything right with you anymore."

Seeing the anguish in his eyes, she reached for him. "You are having as much trouble with this whole thing as I am. I came here wanting to see if we can work through this somehow." She gave him a wry grin. "Brad read me the riot act the other day."

His expression brightened and he reached for her hand. "Me, too. But he was right about everything. I need to listen to you."

"And I need to understand where you're coming from." Her breath seemed to be stuck in her throat at his touch, the encouragement shining in his eyes.

"Why don't you start? I promise to listen." He led her to the sofa.

She eased down beside him, acutely aware that he still held her hand, his touch so warm.

"I am having trouble accepting what happened, but you already know that."

He sandwiched her hands in his. "I understand."

"But finding out about Deidre, then being left out of your plans for Summer, made me feel worthless, not really part of our marriage anymore. As long as we've been married, I have supported you, been there for you during all your business ups and downs. Yet, when it came to the most important part of our lives, you decided to go it alone."

"I see that now. I really do. I did try that day on Skype, but it didn't work out..." He tugged her fingers closer into the palms of his hands. "Carolyn, I want to explain something that might help you understand what I was feeling and thinking."

The look of vulnerability in his eyes touched her. Lucas had always seemed so in charge, so capable of taking care of anything. Yet now she saw the exhaustion in his eyes, the worry lines around his mouth. She didn't say a word while she waited for him to continue. Her only movement was to gently squeeze his hand.

Lucas took a deep breath to steady his racing heart. Looking into her clear blue eyes, he was reminded of the day they met. He'd been waiting for an excuse to talk to her, and her math problems gave him an opening. He still remembered how she chewed her lip as she listened to him, the way she was doing now.

"You and I have wanted children all our married lives, and I was so certain that we would have them. Then, when it became clear that we couldn't, I was as brokenhearted as you were. The only difference was that I felt I needed to be strong for you, to protect you from the pain of knowing there wouldn't be a baby for us. I came home every day, saw the sadness in your eyes and felt helpless to do anything to ease your sorrow."

"You have no idea what it was like, because you were busy or away from home," she said, tears shining in her eyes.

He touched her cheek, wiping the damp spots with his fingers. "I left you to fend for yourself because I wasn't doing well with it, not just for me but for you. I wanted you to have a baby even more than I wanted a baby for me."

"But you didn't tell me that. You left me to believe that I was the one suffering the most, facing up to my sadness."

"That's where I went wrong. I should have talked to you about my pain, my loss, instead of shielding you from it. I believed I was doing the right thing, but I realize now I wasn't. Carolyn, there hasn't been a day that I didn't wish with all my heart we had a child, our child," he said.

"We should have been more open about our feelings," she said. "When you found out that Summer was your child, I needed you to understand how I was feeling. Not just the sense of betrayal but also how left out I felt by your need to charge ahead and do what you believed was best."

"As difficult as this is for me to say, I was so happy to learn that we had a child. I know I handled it badly, but all I wanted was for us to be a family. I had a child who could make that happen, who we could share. The circumstances were not what I would have wished for. But in my mind, it was the next best thing. That's why I rushed into it, organizing everything, thinking that I could fix your loneliness, your need for a child simply by taking charge of Summer's life."

She nodded slowly as her eyes moved over his face.

He felt her gaze like a blessing, a loving thought exchanged between them. "I could have waited and I should have. I should have left with you that first day so we could talk this over. It was so stupid of me. And the worst of it is that I can't go back and fix any of it. I can't take back your pain at feeling left out or the loneliness my crass behavior caused you." He squeezed her hand gently, willing her to believe him. "I can only try and make it up to you now."

He wanted to pull her into his arms and kiss her, show her how much he loved her. But he was afraid that if he moved too fast, she would feel he was pressuring her. He didn't want that. Never. "I don't have the words to explain my behavior. It was wrong of me to make you feel so alone. Since you've been gone, I wake up every morning facing an empty bed. I can't go on like this. The long nights of lying awake, missing you. No morning talks. No discussions about our days. We belong together. There's never been anyone for me but you. Only you."

"Oh, Lucas..." She moved closer to him.

He closed his eyes in torment. He had to get this right. He had to. "And it's because I love you that I'm willing to accept whatever it is you decide you want. I'm here for you. I've tried to make it clear how I feel, how sorry I am. I won't pressure you into a decision about us. I want you to know I feel powerless to change how you feel about what I've done to you."

Lucas fought the urge to crush her to his chest, to plead with her to move home. But if there was one thing he'd learned through all of this, it was that he had to give Carolyn time to accept what had happened and how sincere he was in trying to make amends. "I would like for us to go away together. So much has happened since Boston. I really believe that if we spent time together, really shared our feelings about everything that has happened, we can find our way back to each other. I've already talked to Brad and he's willing to take over for me. I promise to never touch my business cell phone from the minute we leave here until we get back."

He stopped, confused by the look on her face. Was she crying? "Oh, Carolyn, darling, I didn't mean to make you cry. I really wanted to do something nice for you, spend time with you, but if you don't want to'"

"I do," she said quickly.

He held his breath, uncertain as to what to do next. "Are you sure?"

"Yes, I am. More than anything we need to work things out between us."

His throat thick with emotion, he pulled her close and kissed her gently and with so much bottled-up feeling he thought he would burst with happiness. When her arms moved around his neck, he took her face in his hands and kissed the last traces of tears from her cheeks. "Carolyn, whatever happens from here on, we're in this together."

His cell rang, startling both of them. Holding her close, he pulled the phone from his pocket. The caller ID showed the kindergarten he'd hope to enroll Summer in. "Sorry, but I need to take this call. It's about Summer's kindergarten. Do you mind?"

For a moment Carolyn hesitated, her teeth biting her lower lip. "No. Go ahead."

Thankful for Carolyn's support, he answered the phone.

"I'm sorry, Mr. Turner, but we won't be able to offer your daughter a place at our facility because we don't have the space for her. I can leave you on the list and if there's a cancellation, we could see about fitting her in."

He gave a sigh of disappointment. "I'm sorry to hear that. I was hoping you would be able to accommodate her. Thank you for informing me of your decision."

He ended the call and put the phone away.

"What happened?" Carolyn asked.

"I was trying to enroll Summer in a kindergarten recommended to me. They don't have an opening, at least, not now. Maybe later."

"How soon do you need a kindergarten? I understood that Lisa was staying on with you to give Summer lots of time to adjust to her new life here."

He grimaced as he leaned forward resting his elbows on his thighs. "Lisa's not going to be here much longer."

"Why?" Carolyn asked, curious as to why the nanny would be leaving before Lucas had everything in place. But maybe he had found a pediatrician and a dentist and all the other things Summer would need to be healthy and happy. She wanted to be part of that, part of putting Summer's life together here in her home.

The thought warmed her and frightened her at the same time. Yes, she'd wanted to be involved, and she wanted what was best for Summer.

"Lisa has a job near where her mother lives. I hate to let her go, but feel I have no choice. It's been difficult even with her here, I have no clue how I'll manage when she's gone."

"And there is a problem over the kindergarten?"

"More like several problems. No kindergarten arranged yet. I haven't been able to spend the time to get Summer settled the way I'd planned, what with work commitments. Worst of all, I have to tell Summer that Lisa is leaving. I don't know how to do it, and I'm afraid that she will be so unhappy without Lisa..."

She saw the raw pain in his eyes, the way he seemed so lost and alone. Forgetting her own concerns, she said, "Summer will be upset. You can't avoid that. She's a strong little girl, but to be losing the one person who has been with her, who was there from the beginning, will be very painful."

"Lisa and I are going to talk to her about all this tomorrow morning. I'm worried about her reaction. Lisa is upset over leaving Summer but feels that she has to take this job offer. I don't know what I'll do if Summer…"

"That's awful," Carolyn said, imagining how hard it might be for Summer to get over losing Lisa.

"I have to find someone to replace Lisa. I don't see where I can have someone hired in enough time to work with Lisa before she leaves. I mean, I can't be careless with this decision. The nanny has to be someone who is right for Summer."

"What do you believe is the best answer for Summer?" Carolyn asked, seeing the defeated look in her husband's eyes.

Lucas took her hand. "I wish I could answer that without making it sound as if I called you here because I am desperate and you're the only person I can trust. Although that is the truth. There is no one I can call on to help me but you." He got up, his body tense as he clenched his hands and paced the room.

She went to him, her heart melting. She'd been so absorbed in her own problems, her own feelings of loss and anxiety, she'd failed to realize that Lucas was struggling, too. Only he had a child to care for, regardless of how he was feeling. "What is it you want from me?"

"Carolyn, I have no right to ask this. You have had a real hard time because of me. But I want Summer to be happy. Yet I'm worried about her ability to cope with another loss in her life."

His hand moved up her back, around her shoulders, pulling her into the safety of his arms as they stood together at the entrance to the living room, the room where they'd made the decision to buy their home. The memory of those early days of love and caring, and their dream of children filling every room, made her loss even stronger. Overcome with emotion she turned to face him, and the love in his eyes stole her thoughts.

"Would you be willing to be here while we talk to Summer? Summer really likes you. She might feel less upset if you were with her. It's asking a lot, I know."

Seeing the agony etched on his face, Carolyn had to look away. Her knees shaking, she made it to the sofa in the living room, thankful to be able to sit. Lucas followed, easing down beside her.

"Talk to me, Carolyn," he said, his words coming out in a hoarse rasp.

Lucas's body was so close to hers, his heat surrounded her, his hands offering her strength and certainty.

Yet as she sat next to the man who had caused her so much agony, listening to his concern for Summer, she was at a loss as to what to do. If she refused to help him and walked out, their marriage would be over. If she stayed and helped him sort out his problems, she would once again be putting his needs ahead of hers. Rather than resolving their issues, she would be choosing to smooth things over for Summer's sake.

Looking around at all the toys, the books, all the things that made a little girl happy, she realized that she had no right to withdraw her support. Not if it meant that someone as precious as Summer could benefit from her help.

Summer did not deserve to be caught between them. She was a little girl who had lost her mom, the worst thing that could have happened to her. Now Summer was about to lose the second most important person in her life. "I'll stay. I'll be here when they come back."

He took her in his arms, kissing her so gently and with so much slow-burning passion, she was lost in his embrace. Wrapping her arms around him, she stroked his face, returning his kisses, her body arching to his. "Carolyn, I want to make love to you right this minute. Is that what you want?" he asked.

"Yes," she breathed, her hands moving over his chest.

Sighing deeply, he whispered, "We would be upstairs now if I didn't know that Summer and Lisa could be home any minute. But if we weren't facing this situation." He leaned back, pulling her into the crook of his arm, easing her head onto his shoulder. "I am so glad you're here with me."

For the first time in a long while, she felt hope flooding through her. "Summer deserves all the love and caring we can give her," she said, feeling the impact of her words, the love growing in her heart for Summer.

Lucas hugged her close as he led her to the kitchen, walking side by side as they'd done so often before. "Let's have a cup of coffee to celebrate. I'd like to have something stronger, but that can wait until we're alone."

The door to the garage opened. Summer stood there staring at them. "Daddy!"

CHAPTER NINETEEN

Summer raced in, trailing a plastic grocery bag behind her. "We got Cheerios. Lisa says they're good for me. Do you like Cheerios?" she asked, coming to a halt in front of Lucas as she dropped the bag and put her arms out to him.

"I love Cheerios. We'll have them for breakfast, will we?" he asked, lifting her into his arms and kissing her cheek.

"We can have them now," Summer said, planting a big noisy kiss on Lucas's cheek.

He hugged her, his arms cradling her body as he swayed back and forth. "We can do whatever you want, Summer girl."

Summer spotted Carolyn and leaned back in her father's arms. Her eyes widened. "Do you want to make peanut butter sandwiches?" She wiggled out of her father's arms to go to Carolyn. "I help Lisa, but after that we could make some sandwiches," Summer said, putting her tiny hands on her hips, the way Lucas did so often.

Carolyn, her heart filling with love for the little girl who had made her husband so happy, glanced at Lucas. "Like father, like daughter?"

"Oh. You mean this," he said, resting his hands on his hips. "Exactly."

Lucas's smile radiated happiness. "She's amazing, isn't she?"

"Come on." Summer took Carolyn's hand, leading her to the fridge and opening the door, peering inside before pulling out a jar of peanut butter. "You get the bread."

"Are we being just a little bossy?" Lisa said as she entered the kitchen, her arms full of grocery bags.

"Let me do that," Lucas offered, taking the bags from her and placing them on the counter. "I'll get the rest of the groceries out of the car."

Turning to Lucas, Lisa said, "Can you take Summer out with you for a few minutes?"

"Absolutely. Summer, Daddy needs your help with the other groceries." He held out his hand.

"Yeah!" Summer raced past Lisa, red curls circling her head.

"Thanks," Lisa said, nodding at Carolyn. "It's nice to see you."

"It's nice to see you, too." Carolyn helped take the groceries out of the bag feeling more relaxed than she had in weeks. Was it being back in her house again, or was it simply being with Lucas?

She stopped to consider, a bag of Oreo cookies in her hands. It wouldn't be her kitchen again until she could accept everything that had changed these past weeks, changes that both she and Lucas had to cope with if they were going to be part of each other's lives.

With Summer out of the house for a few minutes, she turned to Lisa. "Lucas tells me you're going back to Concord soon."

Lisa hesitated for a few seconds. "Yes. I'm worried about

how Lucas will manage. I've gotten to appreciate him. He's kind and considerate, and he is a great dad. The only reason I feel I can leave is that Summer is perfectly happy here with him. At first, it didn't go so well, but now I have no doubt that everything will work out. The only other thing I wish for Summer is that she have a new mom," Lisa said, a knowing look in her eyes.

"That would be really nice for Summer," Carolyn said, feeling a connection to Lisa who cared so much for the little girl.

"Carolyn, you and I don't know each very well, and we got off to a rough start. If I caused you pain over what I said, I want you to know it was never intended to hurt you."

"You were going through a difficult period, too," Carolyn offered.

"I was in shock after Deidre's death. She was my employer, but she was also my friend. She was a good mother and one of the best people I ever worked for. I miss her. She did everything she could to give Summer a good life, and that included providing for her should anything happen." Lisa chewed her lip in concentration. "And I want you to know that if Deidre had loved Lucas, she would have said something to me. She certainly would not have allowed him to walk out of her life."

"I appreciate you saying that. It's been so hard…"

"I can only imagine. But if I were you, I'd put my trust in Lucas. He's a good man. I'll miss him as well."

Carolyn glanced at Lucas as he came into the kitchen carrying grocery bags, Summer following along behind him. What had he felt when he realized that Deidre chose to keep him out of his daughter's life? That phone call saying that he was Summer's father had to have been very difficult in ways Carolyn could only imagine.

How must it feel to learn that you had a child you didn't know existed when you wanted one so badly? All the lost chances to be with your child, hold her, watch her take her first steps, be there when she went to day care, dream of her future.

"Carolyn!" Summer called from her perch on the edge of a chair at the table. "I need you."

"The queen has spoken," Lucas said, putting the last bag on the counter. "I've learned that resistance is futile," he said, winking at Carolyn.

Carolyn looked into his eyes as he towered over her, his closeness framing her thoughts. She loved this man. She'd loved him since that day in high school. "Can we talk a little more about going away together?" she whispered.

His face brightened. His smile widened. "You mean it?"

"Yes, I do," Carolyn said, leaning close to him, breathing in his scent, feeling at peace and at home in his world.

He picked her up and swung her around, holding her as they danced around the kitchen. "You have made me the happiest man on the planet. We can go anywhere you want," he said, kissing her lips, hugging her body to his.

"No! Don't take my daddy! No!" Summer screamed, racing to her father, pushing on Carolyn, pinching and crying. "Go away!"

It wasn't the pinch that hurt so much as the feeling of separation that rocked Carolyn. Summer's fierce response made Carolyn feel isolated and in need of reassurance. But by Summer's fierce response it was obvious how frightened she was of losing her dad.

Lisa glanced from Carolyn to Lucas and moved quickly, picking Summer up in her arms, patting her back and trying to soothe her. "There, it's okay. You shouldn't pinch anyone, Summer. That's wrong."

"I didn't mean to." Summer stuck her thumb in her mouth as Lisa picked her up. "I want Mommy," she whispered, her tear-stained face looking into Lisa's.

"It's going to be all right. You'll see," Lisa said, her pleading glance reaching across the room to Carolyn.

What should she do? Should she offer to take Summer and soothe her? Or would that simply make things worse? Undecided, she stood rooted to the spot.

Summer began to cry again. Squirming, she stretched out of Lisa's arms, reaching for her father. "Daddy," she pleaded as big sobs shook her body.

Lucas took her in his arms, moving away from Carolyn in his eagerness to soothe Summer.

Carolyn watched helplessly as Lucas cuddled Summer, swaying with her as she sobbed into his neck. "I'm sorry. I didn't mean to upset her." Carolyn said, struggling to maintain calm, to not cry herself. Everything had been going so well, so much better than she could have hoped.

Lucas gave her an anxious smile. "This has happened before. She'll be all right in a few minutes."

Summer glanced at her suspiciously, sniffling and clutching her father's shirt. "You can't have my daddy," she said, a dark frown on her face.

Lucas felt trapped between his wife and his daughter. He'd never been in this situation before, where everything hinged on how he behaved and whether or not Summer could be convinced to let Carolyn be around him.

He could see the hurt look on Carolyn's face and wanted to hold her and reassure her that she was in this with him. They were a team. He had this moment of opportunity, one he wouldn't let get away from him now that he was so close to having Carolyn in his life once again. "Lisa, can you take Summer for me?"

Lisa put her hand on Summer's back, speaking gently to her. "You come with me, sweetie. We'll play dump trucks in the living room. You like driving them over the carpet. I think there's a bunch of new building blocks in the garage. Why don't we get those?"

Summer's sobs faded to soft hiccoughs. "I want to stay with Daddy." She nestled into his shoulder.

Lucas struggled to figure out what to do. He didn't want to upset Summer, but he couldn't let Carolyn feel left out.

He couldn't believe Carolyn had agreed to go away with him. He'd started out today fully prepared to accept that Carolyn and he were finished, but now, with her willingness to be with him, everything had changed.

"Summer, Daddy really needs to talk to Carolyn. I need you to go with Lisa, just for a few minutes. I won't be long, okay?"

Summer snuggled closer into his chest, her suspicious glance still on Carolyn.

Carolyn moved quietly away from them, over toward the kitchen table. "I'm going to sit here for a little while, Summer. You and Daddy talk a bit. You love your dad, and he loves you." She sat at the table, her eyes meeting his, his heart flipping sideways at the look of consolation on her face.

She understood what was going on and had decided to remove herself from the situation. It had been clear from Carolyn's expression that she'd been hurt by Summer's abrupt response, but she'd recovered and had put Summer's needs first.

Looking into her eyes he couldn't remember a moment when he loved her more than he did right now. Seeing her like this, cold reality hit him. He didn't deserve this woman who loved so deeply, who cared with her whole heart. But if he had a chance to keep her, he would love her unconditionally forever.

"Or I can go out into the garden, look at the fishpond and see if the bird feeders need filling while you talk to your dad. Would that be better?" Carolyn asked, smiling warmly at Summer.

Lucas could have hugged her for being so kind, for helping him manage the situation. He mouthed, "Thank you."

She nodded, a small smile starting at the corners of her mouth. "I'll also check for bunny rabbits while I'm in the garden."

"Bunny?" Summer asked, brightening, a look of interest on her face. "Where's the bunny?"

"I'm not sure," Carolyn said, "but maybe if I take a carrot out to the garden, he'll come to see me. We have a small shed at the back where I keep my gardening tools. Maybe he's there. What do you think?"

Summer wiggled out of her father's arms and came to Carolyn. "What's his name?"

"He doesn't have a name yet. He's big and brown, and he loves lettuce. I usually buy lettuce just for him. But why don't you and I see if we can find him, and in the meantime, you can come up with a name for him. How would that be?"

Summer fidgeted for a moment, looked over her shoulder at her father before turning back to Carolyn. "I can find the carrots in the fridge. You want to come with me?"

Carolyn's smile was bright as she looked across the room into Lucas's eyes. Their eyes held. His heart swelling in his chest, he whispered, "I love you."

"I love you, too," she whispered back.

"What are you saying to Daddy?" Summer asked, a small frown forming between her blue eyes.

"Saying? I'm telling your daddy something really special."

Carolyn laughed, the upbeat sound filling the kitchen, a sound Lucas had feared he would never hear again.

Lucas couldn't help but smile as he followed Carolyn and Summer out into the garden. Hanging back just a little, giving the two people he loved most in this world a chance to be together, he felt at peace and happier than he could remember.

Carolyn walked with Summer out to the rear of the garden, hoping that the rabbit would be somewhere near the shed. That's where she'd last seen him. "Summer, what do you think would be a good name for the bunny?" she asked as she searched the area just beyond the pond for any sign of the rabbit.

Summer held the carrot like a sword. "I'd like to call him Sam," she announced. "I would like him to be Sam."

"Sam it is," Carolyn said, still searching for any sign of the rabbit. As they neared the shed, she noted a small shift in some of the huge leaves of the Hostas along the back fence.

"Maybe Sam likes a cool spot, especially on a hot day like this," Carolyn said, moving closer to the large leaves. Pushing one slowly aside, she saw the rabbit crouched under the leaves, his nose sniffing the air, his eyes alert.

"There he is," Carolyn whispered, pointing toward the bunny that looked ready to leap away.

"Can I play with him? Can I hold him?" Summer asked in an exaggerated whisper as she held out the carrot.

"Probably not today," Carolyn said, wanting to hug Summer to her and never let go. She'd never known a moment with so much emotion in it, never imagined that this was what it felt like to love a child and to do something so simple as to search through the garden for a rabbit. She wanted many, many more moments like this.

Glancing at Lucas, seeing the adoring look on his face, she knew beyond a shadow of a doubt she couldn't let go of any of this, no matter what it took. As she stood there, waiting for the rabbit to leap away, she realized in that instant she loved this little girl with all her heart.

The rabbit darted sideways and disappeared farther into the flower bed. "He's gone!" Summer said, charging toward the spot where he'd been. "Let's go," she yelled to Carolyn as she scrambled through the wide, green leaves, making them sway and bend.

"You won't be able to catch Sam. He's faster than either of us."

Summer stopped. "Where did he go?"

"I have no idea. But he likes my backyard so he'll be back soon."

"Yours?" Summer asked, coming to a full stop, making the giant leaves shudder.

Carolyn took a deep breath, aware that Summer might not realize that this was her home, as well. Feeling she had no choice but to answer, she said, "I live here."

Summer put her thumb in her mouth, turning in a wide arc. "Where? Where do you live? In there?" she asked, pointing to the shed.

How should she handle this? Summer only knew about her dad and Lisa being in the house. What would happen if she told Summer the truth? And was it the truth? Did she intend to return to her home, regardless of Summer's response to her?

Anxiety tightening her tummy, she smiled as she leaned closer to Summer and said, "I live in this house. This is my garden."

"No. You don't. Daddy does and Lisa. Not you." Summer scowled at her. "We live here. Not you."

Had Lucas not said anything to his daughter about her?

About their life together? How could that be possible? She glanced at Lucas, as he walked toward her. She struggled not to cry.

"Summer, why don't you go in and get Lisa to give you some Cheerios as your snack?" Lucas asked, taking Summer's hand and leading her toward the door.

Carolyn sought the bench seat at the corner of her garden and sank unsteadily onto its cool surface. Hurt moved through her, betrayal ground its way into her heart.

Why hadn't Lucas mentioned to Summer that she lived here? Had he assumed she wasn't coming home again? Her stomach ached with anxiety and disappointment. She had to get out of here, away from all this. Coming here had been a huge mistake. She'd slip around to the front of the house, grab her purse and leave.

Out of the corner of her eye, she saw Lucas return, his long stride bringing him close to her. It was too late for her to escape, and as she met his gaze, she really didn't want to. She'd made a mistake, assumed too much, and now she had to face her actions because of it.

As he made his way around the perennial bed she'd planted last year, his eyes on her, she steeled herself for the inevitable confrontation. "Why doesn't Summer know who I am and that I live here?"

He stopped a couple of feet from her. "Carolyn, I wasn't sure if you planned to come back, or if I could convince you to return. Summer has had such a confusing time these past weeks, so many things happening in her life, I felt it best to only tell her the things that I was certain about."

He was right, but it didn't matter. Feelings of loss, a strange emptiness tumbled through her. "I wasn't here because you wouldn't include me. It was your choice, not mine. Now your daughter is upset that this is my home as well as hers. You wanted my help, but how can I help if Summer doesn't want me here?"

His eyes searching hers, he said, "I had to make a decision about who was in her life when we arrived here. She was crying and upset. I'd already messed up badly where you were concerned. From what I could tell, there was no chance that you wanted to be part of our lives. It wasn't a decision meant to hurt you. It was a decision made to offer my daughter as stable a life as possible under the circumstances."

He softened his tone as he moved to the bench beside her. "For now, you're someone she likes and can play with. I didn't take it any further than that because I didn't want to disappoint her."

"Why didn't you ask me if I wanted her to know that I lived here?" Carolyn demanded, aware of how unreasonable she sounded but not able to stem the accusation.

"Because we aren't together anymore, Carolyn. We're trying to figure things out, and I really believe we will. But if you weren't coming back, then what would be the point in telling Summer who you really were? If I told her, only to have you decide not to return home, how would Summer cope with that? It's clear she likes you, but if she lost you, too..."

His words hung in the air between them.

Her heart pounding in dread, she said, "Lucas, if only we'd waited and worked out the details of taking her into our lives... All of this would have turned out so differently."

"Yeah..." He sighed as he reached for her hand. "What do we do now? What do we tell her? Whatever we tell her now won't be easily changed without making her upset."

As she looked at her husband, she had to admit that she was to blame here, as well. She and Lucas had to fight for their marriage. They'd never had to before this, but now everything hinged on both of them seeing what they were about to lose. "There's no point in rehashing the past where Summer is concerned. We both should have found a way to talk to each other about this."

His eyes searched her face, his gaze filled with love and longing. "All I've ever wanted is you, Carolyn, I can't help believing that, if we work on it, we can be happy again." He eased closer, the scent of his skin intoxicating. "We can be a family."

CHAPTER TWENTY

Lucas couldn't stop himself from putting his arm around Carolyn's shoulders. He needed to touch her, to feel her close to him while he waited for her to speak. What would she say? Would she feel pressured by Summer's needs to answer him before she was ready? But she'd come here to see him, and that had to mean she wanted to work things out.

"Carolyn, please believe me when I tell you I've changed. This does not have to be resolved right this minute. I dragged you into my problem of finding someone to replace Lisa. That wasn't fair."

"When you say you made your decision about me and my role here so as not to confuse Summer, I believe you. But if we don't decide what we're doing, how we're going to live, we'll confuse her even more."

His heart sank to his stomach. Was she saying that they couldn't fix their differences over Summer? Each time he saw Carolyn with Summer he was more and more certain that she was falling in love with their child. "Then what do we tell

Summer when she asks who you are? Do we say you're a friend? If we aren't getting back together, will you still want to be part of Summer's life? You have to help me here, Carolyn. I'm worried about so many things at the moment."

She stood before him, her face tilted up, a sad smile hovering on her lips. "I love you, Lucas. You have no idea how afraid I was to come here."

He started to interrupt, eager to explain she needn't be afraid of him, but she put her hand over his mouth to stop him.

"Lucas, we can't let our marriage go. We've been through a rough patch, but I have to believe we can work this out."

"Carolyn, the truth is this. I don't deserve your kindness and caring. But if you're willing to work on this, I will do whatever it takes to have you back here in my life."

He drew in a deep breath to ease the thundering in his chest. "We can do this, but we have to be clear what is going on in our lives where Summer is concerned. If there is one thing I've learned in the short time she's been with me, it's that she has to feel safe, to know that people love her. And we still have to get through Lisa's return to Concord and how Summer will cope with that," he said, pulling Carolyn's hand closer to his chest in an attempt to draw her to him. Holding her close, soaking up her warmth, he whispered, "I wish I'd listened to you. If I had, and we'd worked out a way to put our family together, none of this would have happened."

"I doubt very much that any child could lose their mother and not have issues that needed to be dealt with."

He was so thankful for her words. But not nearly as thankful as he felt with her beside him, talking with him, sharing her thoughts. "Are you ready to be a full-time mom? Ready to forgive me for screwing everything up? If we are going to be with each other, we need to figure out how that will work, at least, as much as we can. I realize we won't get everything right, but if we can find a way to be happy as a family..."

He had to find out what would happen next. "What do you want to do? I really want you to tell me what you think would work out best for you, for all three of us."

She didn't say anything for so long he began to panic. What was she thinking? What would he do if she didn't feel she could be part of his life?

Steady. Trust yourself. Trust her.

Her eyes met his. He knew by her expression that she'd made up her mind. His body felt drained, finished.

"Lucas, I don't want to rehash the past few weeks and what's gone on between us. You're right when you say we need to decide what we're doing, both for us and for Summer. Especially Summer."

She looked up into his face and it was as if the sky had brightened.

"What you did hurt me so much. But what you said is true. It was years ago, and I believe you when you say you didn't continue to see Deidre. I want to be with you. I want us to be a family."

He wanted to yell for joy as he wrapped his arms around her and kissed her face, her eyes, her lips, while his hands roamed over her back, down her body. Her sudden intake of breath fanned his desire. "I've missed you. Every day. Every minute of every day." He smoothed his hands over her body, feeling all the familiar spaces, her curves, the bony crest of her collarbone. He loved all of it.

"I missed you, too...so much. It's been awful being without you. It was so strange to come to my house, see things being done differently and realize that if I didn't work things out with you I would not be coming to this house, our home, ever again."

"So, what do we do now?"

"Can we think of something, some way to spend time together as a family? Away from here? Away from all the reminders of what we nearly did to each other?" Carolyn asked, letting her fingers play along the open neck of his shirt, her touch making him wish that there was no one here but them.

"We could always spend a day with Summer at a theme park where she could play. We could watch her be happy. If she asks who you are, we can say that you and I are her family."

"How do we know what she'll ask when we go back into the house?" Carolyn asked.

"We don't," he said, running over the possibilities, all the while distracted by the way Carolyn's body fitted along his, the scent of her hair, the warmth of her skin. "Maybe we should go in now and tell her who you are. Why you're here."

"And what if she is so upset she can't be soothed? What if she can't accept me as part of her life, not to mention the idea that I would be her mother? Maybe we should wait for a little while until she's more settled?"

Lucas met Carolyn's anxious gaze and knew only one thing. He and Carolyn would once again be in the same bed tonight. Whatever needed to happen, whatever explanations were necessary, he would not live without her for another night. "I'm going to talk to Summer about this. I'm going to explain who you are, how important you are to me, how much I love you. And then I have to have faith that our daughter will be okay with it."

Carolyn felt a shiver of anxiety. What if what Lucas wanted to do turned out to be a catastrophe, with Summer inconsolable and calling for her mother? "There has to be a better way. I mean we need to find a way to convince Summer that I'm not taking her mommy's place and that she can feel safe." Worried, she snuggled against Lucas.

"Wish you and I could stay like this, have nothing to think about or worry over for at least a few days." He leaned closer, kissing her lips, awakening her need for him, for all they had missed while living separately.

"Wish we could, too..." She turned to him, catching the look in his eyes, a look of devotion that swept through her heart. She sat up straight, suddenly alive with an idea. "What if we took Summer to Disney for a vacation, even just a couple days? We could do it right after Lisa leaves so that Summer has something fun to do. It might make losing Lisa a little easier for her. That way she wouldn't feel she was losing you when we talk casually about me coming home, and she sees how much fun the three of us can have as a family. If we do this right she will not feel left out or threatened by me being around."

Every ounce of Lucas's attention was focused on Carolyn, making her feel cherished and cared for. "You are a genius," he said enthusiastically. "That would work out perfectly. I'll book us into the Disney resort in Florida. We will have so much fun, the three of us." He pulled her to her feet and walked with his arm around her shoulders as they walked toward the house. "Holding you, having you here with me feels so good," he murmured into her hair as he opened the door into the house.

Their entrance into the family room was met with a squeal of delight from Summer. "Daddy! Lisa and I need to show you something." She took his hand, pulling him into the living room. "See!"

"See what?" he asked, searching the lawn.

"Right there." Summer pointed toward the hibiscus bush near the corner of the flower bed in front of the window. The rabbit, his nose wiggling, was peering out from under the shrub. "I love him. Can he be my rabbit?" she asked, her face turned up to her father.

Love overflowed his heart. "Yes, he can be your rabbit."

"I've already named him. His name is Sam," she said, a look of mischief in her wide blue eyes.

"Sam. Sounds good to me. What do you think, Carolyn?" he asked as she came up behind them.

Standing beside him, seeing him with his daughter, Carolyn was struck by how much they looked alike.

She glanced around the wide foyer, the long length of window forming one wall of the living room, the dining room beyond the living room, its table set as if waiting for the fun and laughter of a dinner party.

Lucas winked at her. "Are we sure this rabbit is a boy?"

"Not sure. But the name works. If needed we can change the name to Samantha, Sam for short," she said, noting that Summer was suddenly showing a great deal of interest in her. "What do you think?" she asked, leaning down toward Summer.

"Just Sam." Summer shook her fist for emphasis. "The rabbit's mine. He looks really, really hungry. I want to get more carrot and some lettuce and see if he will eat it from my hand," she said, heading back down the hall toward the kitchen. They followed, glancing at each other.

As Carolyn moved toward the kitchen with Lucas, she had the sensation that she was coming home: home to a life of toys everywhere, Cheerios in the cereal cupboard and a little girl who was enthusiastic about everything.

"We're the lucky ones, aren't we?" she said, hugging Lucas close, her smile open, her heart humming. "We are in our home with our daughter."

"Life doesn't get much better than this, Mrs. Turner," Lucas said. "We'll get packed and take Summer away on our first family vacation to Disney."

He pulled her into his arms, kissed the breath from her lips. "Welcome home, my love."

THE END

ABOUT THE AUTHOR

Stella MacLean is a story teller. Simple as that.

An author of books, both fiction and nonfiction, she has served as Writer in Residence at Vancouver Public Library in Vancouver, British Columbia. She loves to travel, spend time with family, along with her husband and her fur babies in her home near the Bay of Fundy in Atlantic Canada.

Stella relishes the hours she spends hiding out in her office making up stories about the lives of imaginary people. Having found love again in the third act of her life, Stella enjoys telling stories about people who find love elusive and complicated, but still try with all their hearts.

Stella's past includes being a registered nurse, from which she has drawn story ideas for several of her books. She went back to university when her children were older and was granted a Commerce Degree, majoring in Accounting, from Mount Allison University in Sackville, New Brunswick, Canada.

Visit Stella's website; www.stellamaclean.com

Subscribe to Stella's newsletter for all the latest news and quick previews of upcoming books and events.

Follow Stella on Bookbub for special offers and new releases

Follow Stella on Amazon for up-to-date information on all her Kindle books.

Connect with Stella on Facebook, Twitter

OTHER BOOKS BY STELLA MACLEAN

Unimaginable

Desperate Memories

Desperate Acts

Falling Prey

NON-FICTION

Living Successfully With Chronic Pain